LOVE BEYOND TIME

LOVE BEYOND TIME

A NOVEL

MEHMET TANBERK

iUniverse LLC
Bloomington

Love beyond Time
A Novel

iUniverse books may be ordered through booksellers or by contacting:

iUniverse
1663 Liberty Drive
Bloomington, IN 47403
www.iuniverse.com
1-800-Authors (1-800-288-4677)

Because of the dynamic nature of the Internet, any web addresses or links contained in this book may have changed since publication and may no longer be valid. The views expressed in this work are solely those of the author and do not necessarily reflect the views of the publisher, and the publisher hereby disclaims any responsibility for them.

ISBN: 978-1-4759-9419-3 (sc)
ISBN: 978-1-4759-9420-9 (hc)
ISBN: 978-1-4759-9423-0 (e)

Library of Congress Control Number: 2013910204

Printed in the United States of America.

iUniverse rev. date: 06/13/2013

Contents

Preface

Near the end of 1999, I was in Sydney at my younger daughter's house with my wife and my elder daughter. After a long and tiring professional life, I was dreaming of rest and not doing anything during my retirement. The big cities of the world were racing each other to celebrate the end of a millennium—and the coming of a new one—with magnificent shows. Sydney was among these cities.

I generally woke early in the mornings and strolled through the city, watching the year-end preparations. One day while I was walking toward Watsons Bay, I found myself on a hill where I could see a panoramic view of the harbor. I watched the sun set over the city skyline. The reddish-yellow lights inspired artistic feelings in me. I was unaware of how long I cruised in the ocean of memories. Everything darkened when the sun disappeared behind a thick flock of clouds. Dark blue and purple clouds replaced the red and yellow ones that had been decorating the sky moments earlier. Far away from the horizon, the clouds turned into a hellish black. I felt the tremors of pessimism in my soul and my flesh. Would I lose all the glitter and the colorful treasures I had gathered during my life? Was life an illusion like a rainbow, starting with bright green and yellow and ending up in blue-purple darkness? I ran home and went to sleep without talking to my kids.

I woke up early in the morning and rushed out to the balcony overlooking the harbor. The sun had not yet risen, but light purple beams ascending from the horizon made the dark clouds visible in the sky. I was just about to fall into deep depression when a bright yellow crown appeared on the hills over the harbor. The sunlight was miraculously recreating nature. Ghost spots on the sea were not floating boats; they were motifs of a silk Hereke carpet. The clouds in the sky were as colorful as the paint on an artist's palette.

My feelings were very different from the previous day. If each setting sun was the preparation for a new morning, humans also should have prepared something different for the next day. Maybe the reason of our existence was nothing more than contributing to the everlasting change of the world or preparing something different within the limits of destiny.

1

The Legend of Coming into Existence

In the realm of divine light the Great Angel was excited. An absolute force was attracting all the angels. Long before the creation of the universe, the angels were like drops on an ocean of divine light, which was an infinite source of energy. Because of its homogeneity, there was no concept of time or place. In this ocean of absolute wisdom and existence, God easily communicated with the angels. The angels were nothing but divine light drops; they were differentiated by the size of their glowing spots. The Great Angel was coming after this reality. When the divine call attracted the angels, they were ready to perceive the message of the Lord:

Oh my angels, you should know I'm a treasure of the unknown.
Although I am almighty, my passion is to be known.
I'll put into existence therefore new universes.
I wish to share my power of creation with humans.
There will be a planet that I simply call earth.
It will be dominated by mankind from their birth.
I will create them by destiny of evolution.
To change the earth, they will be equipped with divine notion.
You are the creature's ocean of the divine light.
You will witness the birth of the universe from first sight.

The angels were curious about humans. The Lord instantly replied to their thoughts. He made them aware of human shapes. They were enchanted by them from the first time they saw their shapes. They begged the Lord to take a human appearance—even spiritually. The Lord intended to make humans loved and respected by the angels. Their wish was answered immediately. In the meantime, the Lord ordered the creation of the universe.

A magnetic field appeared in the ocean of light with the Lord's passion. This field started to suck energy from the ocean and turned into a black hole. Vibrations created by the pressure in the black hole transformed the energy into particles. The angels heard a huge sound, and radiating colors burst out of the accumulated energy. The energy scattered particles that created electrons and protons that would last forever and formed matter. With the assembling of these particles, a new universe was born. The angels were confused. They had never perceived sound or colors before, so they were curious. The Lord explained.

Colors are divine decors of a finite world at best.
They hold the reality of creation's secret.
Mankind will learn from them the story of beginnings
Colors will also define the essence of all things.
Colors will make the world beautifully artistic.
They will make the planet entirely unique.
If humans had never been my beloved creatures,
Would I bother to decorate the world with colors?
Who creates anything that resembles this beauty?
Colors are the real proof of the Lord's unity.[1]

---

1   The chronological order of how mankind learned the secret of all the beginnings through the colors, as between the first and fourth lines summarized:

a) In 1816, lens producer Joseph von Fraunhofer experimented with sodium flame as artificial light. The light ray passing through the prism decomposed and created a color scale on the wall, consisting of red, yellow, green, blue, and purple tones. When he repeated the same experiment, replacing natrium with different substances, he realized that the length of the tones on the wall was changing. This proved that each element had a different color scale.

b) In 1880, Margaret Lindsay Huggins compared the rays of different stars passing

The angels questioned the sound after the colors.

The sound is the hallmark of my will for new happenings.
For a finite world, it is permission for new beginnings.
Vibrations in the universe will form all about matter.
Vibrations in the world make sounds for us to hear.
With sounds, my creatures will understand each other.
Many species will make sounds to come all together .
Sounds will contribute to the evolution of humans.
It will also ease for them to get the earthly notions.
Sound is the way that mankind will find divine beauty.
The Lord will use this language to speak humans directly.[2]

---

through the telescope and found the same color scale, proving that they contained the same elements and came from the same source.

c) In 1920, Edwin Hubble noticed that the length of the red area on the color scale of different stars, which contained the same elements, was also changing. He compared his findings with the star map and found out that the universe was expanding at an accelerated speed.

d) In 1930, Georges Lemaitre reversed this finding and thought that the beginning of the universe might have come from a big bang. There was a prerequisite to Lemaitre's theory. If the universe came from a single bang, there should have been temperature variations in the universe.

e) In 1989, a Cosmic Background Explorer (COBE) was launched into space in cooperation with NASA. With the information from the satellite, a map of the universe was prepared in blue, pink, and purple to indicate the temperature differences.

The ninth and tenth lines depict how the colors prove the Lord's unity. Only one white ray, which symbolizes the divine unity, can be decomposed into many different tones when it passes through the prism, which depicts the world. When they come together, we find the unity of divine existence in the color white.

2   Sound, as a hallmark of new happenings, points out the big bang. In 1964, Arno Penzias and Robert Wilson, from Bell Labs, heard strange sounds in the huge receivers they had installed to record signals from an intra-satellite web. There was no satellite in the direction where the sound signals were received. They turned the antennas in different directions, and the signals continued. After meticulous investigation, they realized that these were fossil sounds remaining from the big bang.

The third and fourth lines point out the importance of the vibrations that turned the particles into atoms at the origin.

In the ninth and tenth lines, sound is used to define music. As an effect of vibration, sound is a physical event and cannot have a psychological impact on living creatures. However, when they are put into musical order, all creatures are affected. In other words, a material impulse in a certain order can turn into spiritual communication. That is why sound is the way to find divine beauty and is the language the Lord uses to speak to all creatures.

During the divine communication between the angels and the Lord, the creation of the universe progressed. The formation was taking place in an environment where divine wisdom and energy (spirit and divine light) existed everywhere. In other words, the universe was overlapping with the ocean. All the protons and electrons were scattered into the universe after the big bang. In spite of the huge distances among them, they acted the same way and turned out to be the helium and hydrogen atoms by the will of the Lord.

Later on, the planets and galaxies came into formation—and the universe started to expand because of the gravity of the ocean of energy surrounding it. The Great Angel was enchanted by this progress and desired to be a part of human evolution. After a while, he would find himself in a finite world without even noticing that the Lord had granted his wish.

2

Birth in the World

In 2638 BC, during the beginning years of the fourth dynasty kingdom in Egypt, pharaohs had absolute power. They were supposed to be the sons of the sun deity. In spite of their undisputed authority, they used to rule the country with justice and rightfulness. Their main assistants in their duties, the queens, were respected by all Egyptians. This esteemed position in the community stemmed from their religious beliefs.

Osiris, the deity of fertility and benevolence, was murdered by the deity of cruelty and aridity. His wife, Isis, revived him and returned him to life. *Ma'at* laws, which were the essential rules of the Egyptian civilization, had also been prepared by a female deity. The pharaohs were obliged to make the Egyptian citizens happy and to find jobs and food for their subjects, according to the *Ma'at* rules. Criminals were punished. Building temples to endure thousands of years was another important duty of the pharaohs. These temples were not only for worshipping. The priests of the temples were educating the children to read, write, and learn the arts (music, painting, sculpture, and science) medicine, mathematics, architecture, and astrology. This social order combined with the fertility of the river Nile to be the foundation of a civilization that would last four thousand years.

Another country shared the fertility of the Nile, but it never reached the level of Egyptian civilization. Nubia was situated on the southern border of Egypt. It was no less rich than Egypt in natural resources. The northeastern part of the country, in spite of some deserts, had rich gold mines. In the southern part, there were forests with valuable timber to make ships and abundant animals for hunting. In central Nubia, two branches of the Nile met and created a fertile land for agriculture and convenient waters for fishing. In spite of these favorable opportunities, they could never establish a civilization like Egypt. Nubians had no rules to provide social order or leaders to apply them. It also lacked the teachers to educate the younger generations. Young girls were being taught housework, and boys were taught to hunt. Women had no social responsibility or much respect in their society. They used to give birth to the children and keep the houses in order. From time to time, kings and princes ruled the country, but they never had much power over the scattered and independent tribes.

Aspelta, one of the chiefs of these tribes, was getting ready for a hunting party. He woke up early in the morning. His men loaded the donkeys with hunting equipment. Aspelta was taking his only son with him. In spite of his eleven years of age, Kumma was a strong and clever boy. His father decided that he was sufficiently mature to meet the wilderness and direct the men. This hunting safari could be a good start.

When preparations were completed, father and son were riding on donkeys in the middle of the group. Aspelta's men surrounded them for protection. Three donkeys were loaded with goats as reserve food in case they did not hunt anything. Their destination was not far from the village. Due to the last days of his wife's pregnancy, Aspelta had not wanted to go too far. They reached the camping place at noon. A river entered the reedy land to form a natural bay; five hundred steps from the shore, there was wood. Between the wood and the shore, the tents were set up in a plain. Aspelta and Kumma sat on rugs under the shadow of a willow tree.

Aspelta said, "This is the first time you have come hunting with me, Kumma. Don't ever take hunting as a simple game. This is a fight for survival. If you underestimate the animals, you can be the hunt. If you overestimate them, you lose your courage and will be in danger. You need to watch where you are, be careful, and use your brain."

Kumma was already watching each detail very carefully, but his father's words had a big impact on him. Aspelta was giving orders to each group of men. Some men would unload the donkeys, place the equipment properly, and set up tents. Others would slaughter the goats and prepare the meal and the fire. Aspelta preferred to watch the latter. One of the goats was brought to a hollow. A man stepped on the animal. Another tried to cut its throat, but he only succeeded after many cruel attempts. The blood from the animal's head poured into the hole. Its rear legs were still moving. Kumma's sadness did not escape Aspelta's attention.

"You should get used to these kinds of scenes, my son. A good hunter must be cruel. You must kill to survive. Otherwise, they may kill you. Don't forget the nature is also cruel."

Aspelta and Kumma had a good rest under the shadow of the trees. A few hours later, the meal was ready. After a delicious lunch, Aspelta started to give new orders. Some men were sent to dig a deep hole close to the shore; others went fishing with spears. Suddenly, one of them threw his spear into the water. Kumma ran toward the shore. When the spear was out of the water, there was a fluttering fish at its sharp end. A few minutes later, other men started to catch fish. Kumma liked fishing. He took a spear and tried to catch one. He failed each time he tried.

He said, "Dad, can I catch fish like your men? Can you teach me how to do it?"

Aspelta said, "You should find out how to catch a fish by your own observations. We mostly stay alone in the wild and cannot always find someone to ask. Find your own way, son."

Kumma realized he wasted his time by trying without observing. He watched the men more carefully. They were holding the spears very close to the surface. He had thrown his spear from a distance and scared the fish. He tried some more times, more carefully, but still failed. He came closer to the hunters and noticed they were throwing the spears a little bit in front of the fish. Other fishermen were walking out of the water. Kumma was up to his knees when he saw a moving shadow beneath the water. Without any rush, he brought the spear as close as possible to the surface and threw it in front of the fish. He could not believe his eyes when he raised the spear out of the water. He had caught the biggest fish of the day.

Some men were cooking the fish while others were placing sharpened sticks vertically into a hole. They covered the top of the hole with wooden sticks, reeds, and grass.

Kumma asked, "What are these men doing, Father?"

Aspelta replied, "Early in the morning—before sunrise—some animals come here to drink water. If we are lucky, we can catch one with our trap."

When dinner was served, they brought Kumma the fish he had caught. It was so tasty. Kumma gained confidence after his catch. He was dreaming of being a good hunter who was capable of hunting anything. After the meal, they set a big fire where everybody would sleep. Some men would stay awake and patrol.

Kumma said, "As you can see, my son, in order to be a good chief, you must think of every detail in advance. You must explain and delegate each the duties you expect from your men."

Kumma gazed at the sky when his father finished talking. He had never realized there were so many stars in the sky. After falling asleep, he dreamed of being torn apart by wild animals. He woke up in a panic. He heard howling. He woke his father and asked about the wild sounds coming from every corner.

Aspelta answered, "The howling is coming from jackals. They should have smelled the blood of the goat we slaughtered. They must be the dark ones that can be found in this area in singles, pairs, and herds. With so many howls, it must be a rather big herd. They do not attack humans if they are not very hungry."

"What if they are very hungry?"

"Then they can be wilder and attack everything."

"Do you mean it's our final hours, Father?"

Aspelta tried to calm his son. "Don't be afraid, my boy. A good hunter must be clever and brave."

After a short break, Aspelta turned to some of his men and told them to take the hide and remaining meat of the goat with them. He chose four of his best archers and gave them bows and plenty of arrows. The other group would stay with Kumma near the fire.

After lighting some torches, Aspelta and his men walked toward some nearby acacia trees. Kumma could see them under the light of the full moon. They hung the hide and the meat on the branches of three tallest trees. Four archers climbed into the trees. The rest returned to the camping site. It did not take long before Kumma noticed the jackals. They were trying to reach the hide and the meat by pushing and pawing each other. A few jackals jumped up and fell down together. The others reached the hide and the meat by trying to eat as much and as quickly as possible. The ones that could not find anything to eat were staring at the camp.

In the meantime, the archers started to shoot the jackals from the trees. The jackals that could not get sufficient meat attacked the wounded members of the herd. Now *they* were the hunt. The men in the camping area had difficulty keeping the donkeys from being scared by the howls. One of the archers fell slowly from the tree, and the jackals attacked immediately. The scream of their friend froze everybody's blood. Kumma felt as if his dream had come true. The other archers tried to shoot as many jackals as they could, but they could not save the life of their friend.

Kumma was very scared and affected by all the things he had witnessed. His only consolation was to be near his father.

Aspelta said, "After I pass away, my son, you will be surrounded by humans who will be more dangerous than the jackals. In order to overcome your rivals, you should divide them by throwing separate food in front of them. Wait behind the traps as we did tonight. At your earliest convenience, kill them one by one without leaving any breathing creature behind. Don't forget how it happened tonight; your first and only mistake becomes your last before dying."

Kumma was not ready to hear that much cruelty. He said, "I do not want to be the chief of the tribe after you, Father."

Aspelta smiled bitterly and said, "That will not save you from death, my boy. Because you are the son of the former chief, nobody would believe you—even if you had wanted to renounce. They will always see you as a threat."

Kumma was about to accept his destiny.

Aspelta said, "Not only that. Neighboring tribes can attack you in animosity. You must be superior to them as well. You can gain most of the instincts and abilities needed to survive during safaris. The jackals we killed tonight were superior to us in quantity and strength, but we won against them with our courage, carefulness, shrewdness, and tricky traps—all which we gained in hunting."

In the morning, Aspelta and his men woke to the voices of messengers from their village. Kumma's mother, Nitokris, was about to deliver her baby. Kumma, his father, and some of the men rode on donkeys and hurried back to the village. When they entered the home, a doctor was waiting for them in front of Nitokris's room. In one corner, a doctor's assistant was preparing hot water. When Aspelta and Kumma reached the bed, Nitokris smiled. She had been encouraged to know that her husband and son would be with her during the birth. Kumma held his mother's hand. She was suffering from the regular pains, but she was smiling.

The doctor asked Aspelta and Kumma to wait on the terrace. Kumma heard his mother's screams but was unable to do anything. An hour later, the doctor left the room. Kumma knew something was wrong because of the man's pale face and trembling voice.

The doctor said, "I do not know how to tell you, Chief Aspelta, but the baby entered the birth channel from the opposite side. We can only save the mother or the baby under this circumstance."

Kumma felt a pressure in his heart. His legs were hardly carrying his body. He had difficulty understanding why his mother should have been sacrificed to save an unborn baby. His father was thinking before answering the doctor's question. Kumma looked at his father with fear and anxiety.

Aspelta turned to his son, put his hand on his shoulder, and said, "Look, my son. The strength and survival of our tribe depends on my offspring. You will take my place after me, but until you grow your own sons, we need more people from our blood. That's why the unborn baby is very important and has to be saved."

Kumma understood what his father meant. He said, "Father, it is not yet definite that the unborn baby will be a boy. If you decide to sacrifice my mother for the baby, I cannot stay with you. To earn a new member of the family, you lose a son. Even worse, you earn an enemy. If you insist on your decision, I will have to join to one of our rival tribes."

Aspelta ordered the doctor to save the mother. He entered the room with Kumma to inform his wife of the decision. The doctor took the knife from his assistant and kneeled between the woman's legs. Aspelta held his wife's right hand and told her they had to sacrifice the baby. After a deadly silence and a scream of pain, the woman turned to Aspelta and said, "No. You cannot kill my baby. I have finally gotten pregnant after so many years. I carried my baby with love and hope. Can a baby who has not seen anything in the world be sacrificed for a woman who has lived so many years? How could one imagine that I would live without my baby? Doctor, please be quick and save my baby."

Kumma and his father sweated. Aspelta nodded his head. The doctor rubbed her abdomen with an ointment to relieve the pain. He took the knife and hid it inside his hand. Inserted his hand into the birth channel without damaging the baby and drove back the knife, cutting the lower part of the woman's body.

Nitokris screamed, and the doctor pushed his hands further inside. He pulled the baby out and placed the baby boy near his mother. She turned to her baby and looked at him.

Aspelta looked at his wife with great admiration. There was no more pain—only happy submission. She turned to Kumma and whispered, "I entrust your brother to you, Kumma. He will grow up without knowing motherly love. You should compensate for my absence."

She shut her eyes. This way, in the world, the Great Angel was born.

Kumma hugged his mother with pain and regret. He put his head on her chest and cried loudly. He recalled the beautiful days full of compassion with his mother. She had asked him to give the same love to his brother in compensation for her absence. How he could do this? His mind was resisting the idea; his heart was holding the baby boy responsible for the death of his mother. On the safari, his father had taught him to stay alone in nature, but he had really stayed lonely in the world.

Kumma did not know how long he cried, but he felt his father's hands on his shoulder. His father dragged him out of the room. When he woke up in the morning, he did not recall anything for a while. When the cruel reality struck his mind, he walked toward his mother's room. His father was inside.

Aspelta hugged his son. Both of them missed the beloved woman.

According to the traditions, Nitokris would be buried first. On the same day, the baby would be given a name. Kumma could not stand to attend and see all these things. He said, "Father, I am not mentally ready for today's funeral ceremony. If you permit me, I'd like to stay alone with my sorrow."

Aspelta called one of the guards and said, "Husen, get ready for a one-day trip with my son."

A few minutes later, the soldier was ready. There were three donkeys— one for Kumma, one for the soldier, and one for the equipment. Kumma preferred to go back to the place where he had camped with his father. They departed early in the morning. The place with the trap hole was convenient for fishing.

Along the way, Kumma watched his surroundings. He was trying to learn new things. When they got closer to the camping area, they had more difficulty seeing the shore through the long reeds and tall acacia trees. When they passed the last hill before the shore, Kumma noticed a small animal near the trap. They sped up. The cover of the hole had collapsed. A gazelle had been pierced by the sharp sticks. Its eyes were open, and it was looking up.

The soldier cried joyfully, "Very seldom can there be such luck."

Kumma and the soldier tied up their donkeys. On his way back to the shore, Kumma saw a little gazelle near the hole. It was looking inside and making low sounds. It could hardly walk; it staggered on its front legs when it tried to run away.

Kumma sat on the closest rock to watch the baby gazelle without scaring it. Suddenly his newborn brother came to mind. He had also lost his mother on the day he opened his eyes to the world. He realized how lucky he was for the time he had spent with his mother. His hatred for his brother suddenly went away. He recalled his mother's last words. His brother was in need of his love. He wanted to go back to his village immediately. The soldier took the baby gazelle in his arms. They rode on their donkeys and turned back. When they reached the village, Aspelta met them.

After Kumma explained their story, Aspelta sent the gazelle to the sheepfold. During Kumma's absence, the funeral ceremony had been completed. His little brother was named Semneh. Kumma wanted to see him. When he got close to him, Semneh smiled. Kumma suddenly knew how much he would love his brother. The pain of a baby gazelle had wiped the rust of hatred from his heart.

3

Fifteen Years Later

Aspelta's village was on a hill. The mud bricks for the houses had been carried by the river and dried in the molds. The roofs were covered by reeds on bamboo sticks. Palm trees and cactuses in front of the houses naturally decorated the village. On the northern side of the village, they had a meadow and a wood. There was a shallow bay just below the wood on the shore of the river. The right side of the village was a farming area. People grew wheat, barley, and grapes on the slopes. Above the wood were the folds for cattle, sheep, and goats.

Semneh woke to the sounds of animals. His brother would take him to the exercise area of the hunters near the river. A lot had changed in the fifteen years since his birth. His father married Nefru, the daughter of a tribe chief on the other side of Nile, and had another son. Nefru had no discrimination among the children and loved Kumma and Semneh as her own. Semneh knew Nefru and Buhen as his own mother and brother.

Kumma took Semneh with him to the hunting exercise. When they arrived, they rested for a while. Kumma would start with archery practice first. There were wooden target boards at different distances. He was among the best archers of his tribe. He easily shot the first and second targets. Hitting the third one had not been difficult either. Kumma aimed the fourth and hit it with his second try. The soldiers were watching him curiously. When he turned to the fifth target,

Kumma stretched the string as much as he could and stopped. He focused his attention on the bow and pulled it a little more. He sent the arrow farther than the board, which was an outstanding achievement.

Semneh was not interested in the distance his brother could reach and wondered why he had not hit the target. According to him, Kumma was a hero for whom nothing was impossible. Kumma decided to train his brother. He gave Semneh a suitable bow. Semneh was stronger than he thought and enjoyed archery. After some time, he called a soldier to take care of his brother. He would practice throwing axes at wooden target boards in the acacia branches. It was more difficult than the first one, but he was talented. Each time he threw the axe, it hit the target. More soldiers were watching him.

Kumma tried more difficult exercises. He started to throw the axe while he was in motion. He threw the axe when running and turning to the opposite side. He tried to shoot the same targets with spears. Finally, he went back to his brother. Semneh was practicing seriously. When he saw his brother, he ran toward him cheerfully. In order to show Kumma his talent, he tried the second and third targets. He could work till evening, but he had to attend lunch with his brother. After lunch, they intended to rest on the grass, but there was a strong wind from the west. They turned back to the village when the wind blew stronger.

At last, they were at home. They were very tired. Semneh watched the sun set in front of his house. A red road over the river reached their village. A few minutes later, a thick cloud blocked the sun. The sky darkened unusually. No villager had ever witnessed such a dark evening. The people gathered in the village square, expecting an explanation. Aspelta could not say anything. That night, they went back to their homes and soon forgot the scene.

Semneh woke up early in the morning. The children and parents would visit Nefru's father. Psamtik was a chief on the other bank of the Nile. They were excited to cross the river on a big raft. They felt like great explorers. When they got on the boat, they stretched a canvas across the mast. A proper wind carried them to the other side in less than an hour.

Psamtik was waiting for them on the shore. He embraced all of them. They walked to the village, which was not far away. When they arrived at the house, Psamtik's wife was on the terrace. Below the terrace, there were mats on the grass with all kinds of food and drink. Everybody was hungry, and they started to eat. After lunch, the children went to sleep while the grown-ups talked on the terrace.

When sun was about to set, a dark cloud—bigger than the day before—appeared and darkened the sky. The wind was blowing so strongly that the villagers had to rush to their homes. Kumma saw something strange in the cloud. There were small particles of gray and dark pink moving like boiling water. The wind continued all night, and Aspelta's family could hardly sleep.

In the morning, they woke to loud screams. Kumma was the first to check on what was going on. He opened the door to the terrace, and hundreds of locusts jumped on him. He tried to protect himself with his fingers. He could not believe what he saw. Thousands of locusts had covered the farms in a gray-pink layer. There was a strange noise coming from the destruction of the crops. It seemed there was no end to the flock of locusts. More insects had gathered on roofs, and most of them collapsed after a while. A new scream burst out from the fold. Animals were running out and breaking down the fences.

Aspelta went out to the terrace and protected himself with his arms. He looked at his village on the other bank of the Nile. The flocks had not yet reached the other side, but there were thousands of black spots. Psamtik followed him and looked at the farms to the west. All the crops had been destroyed. Aspelta, Psamtik, and Kumma went back to the room. They tried to cover the children and women with clothes to protect them and killed the remaining bugs by stepping on them.

In the meantime, Aspelta analyzed the situation. If they did not do something, the flocks would cross the river and damage their farms as well. He said, "Psamtik, I think the best way to fight them is to set fire to the farms where the crops were already damaged. We can stop them and prevent further destruction."

The old man could not think of any other solutions. He approved the idea, but it would not be easy to set fire to the farms.

Semneh said, "My brother can shoot an arrow that far."

Aspelta looked at Kumma suspiciously. In one corner of the house, there was a bow and plenty of arrows. They closed the sharp ends with cotton cloths and dipped them in oil. It was close to sunset, and most of the locusts had landed.

Kumma walked out. Aspelta and Semneh followed him with torches. Kumma climbed on a high rock, took a flaming arrow, checked the direction of the wind, and stretched his bow. He let the arrow go. The first one reached the middle of a farm. Kumma sent more to other farms, and flames rose from the first farm. Some villagers had come to watch Kumma and heard burning locusts. The fire was moving toward the shore. Everything was in order, and most of the people went home.

Kumma, Semneh, and Aspelta decided to go back. On the way, Kumma felt a change in the wind's direction. It was blowing stronger and carrying the flames toward the village. The villagers were in a panic. A spark fell on the roof of the closest house. Soon most of the houses caught fire. All efforts to extinguish them were useless.

Psamtik ordered the villagers to leave their houses and run away with their families. Psamtik and Aspelta did the same.

Aspelta found his raft on the shore. He took his father-in-law and family with him. The raft was crowded, but a favorable wind carried them to the other bank safely and quickly. When they looked back to the west, they noticed the magnitude of the tragedy. The beautiful yellow farms had turned to black ash.

4

Destination Egypt

Setting fire to the farms had saved the other farms from destruction. Aspelta's tribe was among them. In return for their sacrifice, they helped repair the houses and folds. They searched for the animals from the shelters. They filled the molds with mud to make bricks. They cut reeds to cover the roofs. They even gave some of their men to help them.

At the end of these efforts, the accommodation problems were solved. A food shortage was growing. The limited stocks of the eastern tribes could not suffice for both sides.

Aspelta invited the chiefs of the west tribes to a meeting in the afternoon. Psamtik was the oldest of the chiefs. The visitors were welcomed by Aspelta and his sons. Young girls served them drinks of barley and grapes.

Psamtik said, "My dear friends, our people on the west banks had an unforeseen disaster two weeks ago. Our eastern neighbors helped us. I thank them gratefully, but we all know they cannot share their food with us for much longer. Since we lost all our crops and most of our animals, we shall not be able to feed our children and women for very long. We have to find a solution before they starve to death."

One of the chiefs said, "But what can we do if the gods have forgotten us?"

Psamtik said, "When we are in grave trouble and worrying for the days to come, the troops of our northern neighbor, Egypt, live in abundance. According to my knowledge, after old Huni died, the new pharaoh, Snefru, spent all his time making a huge pyramid. He stopped paying attention to the border."

Mirgisseh said, "Psamtik explained our troubles, but does he suggest attacking an Egyptian fortress? If we do so, we must challenge the army of Egypt. Even the number of the soldiers in the fortress is not many; we have no arms to fight. We will not have much hope of winning."

Psamtik said, "Mirgisseh is right. Our chance of winning is very low, but if we don't do anything, our chances for survival are none. Can we grow sufficient crops for winter? Can we replace our lost animals? Can we feed our children without any food? If we had the slightest chance, why should we take such a risk? What can we do now? We can make arrows, bows, spears, and other arms to train our people for a fight?"

Mirgisseh and the chiefs of the western tribes accepted his proposal. The eastern tribes were not eager to take such a risk. They had no food shortage. Some chiefs openly declared this.

Psamtik said, "Our eastern neighbors are right to reject us. We are on the verge of death, and they don't have such problems. No matter what they decide, we have to do something. And if they leave us alone, we can lose the fight or run away. In both cases, the Egyptian forces follow us. They will kill everybody without any discrimination. But if we win in spite of all difficulties, we will be much stronger with the loot we shall acquire. Then the eastern tribes will not be able to live much longer against us. There will not be much change for our fate whether we fight with the eastern tribes or alone."

The eastern tribes started to contemplate. Evening the balance of power between the east and west was important for continuing the present situation. If one side became stronger, the other would not be at ease. Psamtik's words had been effective. They agreed to tackle the problem together. It was unanimously agreed that no chief would assume the responsibility of commanding the joint forces.

Psamtik's younger brother said, "My brother chiefs, I know somebody who is trusted by everybody and talented enough to fulfill the task. I suggest Idenu gives the command."

Idenu had not been noticed previously. He was tall, strong, and about fifty. After his father died, he had spent most of his childhood with his Egyptian mother in a village near Elephantine. He could speak fluent Egyptian. When his mother died, he came back to Nubia. He was not interested in farming or breeding. He went to the Allaki Valley to work in the gold mines. Nobody had heard about him for a long time. When he came back after five years, he married the daughter of a rich farmer. When his father-in-law died, he became a farmer. The chiefs applauded this proposal.

Psamtik said, "Brother Idenu, will you take the command of our joint forces?"

Idenu stood up. "I thank you all for the trust you have placed in me. My farms were damaged by this disaster. It is therefore my pleasure to help you. I need 150 volunteers to train for as long as I see necessary. Additionally, I want sufficient men to make bows, arrows, and spears."

All the chiefs agreed to his conditions. Kumma was one of the first to register. Training the volunteers started immediately in the special field of Aspelta's village. Semneh used to watch them carefully and talk to Idenu.

Ten days later, Idenu invited the chiefs to tell them they were ready. He had one more request. He wanted to take Semneh with him.

Aspelta said, "You already took Kumma. I cannot give two of my sons."

"In this case, I prefer Semneh."

Aspelta had to accept. He thought it could be a good experience for Semneh.

Idenu told his men to load the ammunition and food on fifteen donkeys. The men rode the donkeys and set out on their mission. They followed the coastline until evening each day. On the ninth evening, they arrived at the last stop before the final destination. It was an ideal camping place on a shore where they could fish, find drinking water, and rest under palm trees. In the morning, Idenu took five men.

Idenu said, "Don't move until you hear from me."

While the rest of the soldiers stayed where they were, Semneh and five men followed Idenu. They had not taken any weapons with them; they only had food and water. That evening, they started to climb a slope. When they came to the top of the hill, Semneh could not believe what he saw. The fortress was on an island in the middle of a river. It was encircled by high walls and many soldiers. A thousand soldiers could not conquer this fortress. There was a long distance from the castle to the shore.

Idenu did not hesitate to go. They arrived on the coast. Semneh saw Egyptian barks. These had nothing to do with the rafts they used to cross the river. In the meantime, Idenu was talking to the guards. At the end of their conversation, the guards searched them. Two soldiers led them to a boat. They had to leave their donkeys with the guards. When they arrived at the castle, they were taken to the commander. Semneh was watching them while they talked.

"Commander, I am Idenu from Nubia. Because my mother was Egyptian, I spent most of my youth here after my father passed away."

"What was her name?"

"Her name was Sarah. Our house was behind the folds."

"I think I remember you. My mother had a friend named Sarah. Why did you come here?"

"I have big farms in Nubia, but they were damaged by locusts. In order to save my family from starving, I came here to buy some food if I can. I brought my son and some of my men."

"What would you like to buy, brother?"

"I prepared my list. Take a look if you want."

The commander thought for a moment. He was computing how much Idenu's need would weigh in silver or gold.

Idenu pulled a purse from his girdle with plenty of silver and gold. There was no money in ancient Egypt. People used to barter for goods among themselves. Exchanging goods against gold and silver was more common among the rich. This type of payment was preferred in the unofficial trades.

The commander bowed and said, "Brother Idenu, my name is Reshan. We were your neighbors long ago. I thank the deities that we have met again. I invite you and your men to dinner tonight. All your needs will be ready by tomorrow."

"My dear, I recall that you were a little boy when I left Elephantine. It is marvelous to see you again as the commander of this fortress. Will you excuse us for tonight since we have been on the road for ten days without much rest? Tell your men to give us something from the kitchen so we can go to sleep immediately."

Reshan said, "Soldier, take my guests to the kitchen. Tell the cook to give them whatever they want."

In the kitchen, Idenu put something soft in Semneh's hand and whispered, "Semneh, when I bow my head, put this in one of the pots."

Semneh's heart was pounding. The cook served the soup. He walked to the oven where the meat was served. After getting his soup, Semneh was alone near the cauldron. He put the stuff from his hand in it. He followed the group quickly. Nobody was suspicious. When he came over to Idenu, his hands were still trembling. After picking up their meals, they went to their room. There were mattresses on the floor and a jug on the table with drinking water. Semneh could not sleep for a long time, but he did not ask any questions.

Two hours later, Idenu woke them up. They left the room silently. Most of the candles had gone out. In spite of the moonlight, it was dark. Idenu went into kitchen. The cook was dead. Idenu took five sharp knives from the kitchen. They carefully walked into the other rooms. Idenu's plan had worked successfully. The poison had been effective.

Five of his men wore the Egyptian dresses and walked down to the wharf. They boarded the boat and crossed the river. The guards were all dead from the poisonous soup. Idenu loaded the dead soldiers on a boat and let them float away. The villagers were sleeping. They rode the donkeys back to the other side of the hill where the rest of the men were waiting. Idenu split his men into two groups. Thirty archers would be waiting on the hill. The rest would be attacking the town.

Semneh said, "Let's pick up the animals and food. Why would we kill the people?"

Idenu said, "We can find loot in the homes."

Semneh said, "But those people are our neighbors. There can be women and children in the homes. What threat can they pose for us?"

Idenu said, "If we leave any living souls behind, the pharaoh will send his troops to kill all of us."

Semneh said, "Don't touch the babies. They cannot talk."

Idenu said, "If they lose their parents, they cannot survive and will die in pain."

The soldiers attacked the villagers with axes, knives, and spears.

Semneh could not bear to hear the cries of the slaughtered men and women, but he could not stop the cruel massacre.

In two hours, there was not a living soul in town. Idenu told the archers to come down. All of them started to loot the town. The soldiers went into the homes to find anything precious and killed the survivors.

The Nubian group headed back before sunrise. When they arrived in Nubia, the villagers cheered the victory. The neighbors joined them later.

Idenu and Semneh had become tribal heroes. The loot was distributed in proportion to the number of men each tribe had assigned to the joint force. There would not be any more risk of starvation, and the people were safe.

In the following months, there was plenty of rain. There was no flooding to destroy any crops. People were so happy that everybody in Nubia forgot the past incidents. In other places, people had not forgotten anything.

5

Colors of Civilization

When the pharaoh heard about the looting and massacre at Elephantine, he assigned a committee of military and security officers to investigate. One of two neighboring countries had to have done it—Libya or Nubia.

The mission went immediately to find out the truth. The looted area was on the east bank of the river. An attack from Libya could only be effective from the west. Nubia was behind the massacre. Snefru called an army of twenty thousand soldiers. He assigned one of his sons, Nefermaat, as the commander. The main mission of this army was to occupy strategic points on the border to use as cushion areas for hostile attacks. If possible, the army would also take control of the gold mines in the Allaki Valley. In order to transport the army through the Nile, Nefermaat ordered barks, which carried fifty soldiers in each, to cruise with sails and oars. The fleet came to Elephantine and left some soldiers for protection. The rest continued to Nubia.

In Kumma's village, there was silence. Aspelta was not in the town. He had gone hunting with his youngest son. It was so hot that many people could not sleep till late at night. A cool wind after midnight had put most of them to sleep.

Semneh was awake. He walked out to the terrace. When he looked at the river under the moonlight, he could not believe his eyes. There were so many barks on the river. On the west bank, many soldiers had landed. He realized that the coast of his village was under occupation. He was frightened when he recalled how cruelly they had been in Elephantine. He woke up everybody.

When the women and children saw the fleet, they went back. Kumma and Semneh stayed on the terrace. Shortly after sunrise, all the people in the town gathered in the town square. The Egyptian soldiers proceeded to encircle the people. One of the soldiers wanted to know the chief of the town.

Since Aspelta was away, Kumma spoke on behalf of the town. Kumma and Semneh walked to the middle of the square.

When Prince Nefermaat arrived in the square, six soldiers stood in front to protect him. He looked around, saw Kumma, and said, "Are you the chief of this tribe? Tell them we shall not hurt anybody."

"I am the son of Aspelta. He is not in town. What do you want from us?"

"We shall take the young members of your tribe to Egypt to put them work on the pyramids. Call your men to gather around you. We shall select them."

Kumma's heart was filled with strange feelings. On one hand, he was sorry to leave from his land and friends. On the other hand, he appreciated the attitude of the prince. When Kumma turned to his people to convey the message of Nefermaat, he noticed a shadow behind the closest house. An archer had taken aim at the prince. Kumma stopped, grabbed an axe from the closest guard, and threw it suddenly. The axe hit the archer in the forehead. Everybody was shocked.

Nefermaat had never witnessed such a quick, precise warrior. He put his hand on Kumma's shoulder, looked into his eyes, and said, "You saved my life. You will come to Egypt with me."

Semneh said, "Take me with you, brother."

Nefermaat saw the glitter of wisdom in his eyes. He turned to Kumma and said, "You can take your brother with you if you want."

Semneh ran toward Kumma joyfully. Kumma later learned that

seventeen thousand Nubians had been enslaved in this rally. Most of them were placed in the patrol stations under Egyptian command.

Egypt had taken control of lower Nubia and the gold mines in the Allaki Valley. Some of the Nubians were taken to Egypt. Kumma and Semneh were destined to a different fate.

Semneh and Kumma followed Nefermaat to his boat. When Semneh took a closer look at the boat, he thought he was dreaming. There was a golden sphinx engraved in front. Guards placed the prince in his cabin just before the rudder. Kumma and Semneh were between the prince and the oarsmen. Semneh was watching the cabin of the prince in amazement. A yellow shining sun was attracting attention between the horns of a bull. Just below the sun, a gray bird's wings extended to the edges of the cabin. The upper sides of the wings were in blue and turquoise. The lower sides were red.

Semneh said, "Brother, look at how attractive the colors are."

Nefermaat said, "Come here, young man. What made you so excited?"

Semneh said, "I have never seen such beautiful colors before."

Nefermaat said, "In Egypt, we always search for beauty and express our lust for perfection with colors. Colors are the inspirational power of the deities and the driving force of our civilization. If you like the colors on my boat, you will like Egypt. You will never find such colors in any other place because these are the colors of civilization."

Though Semneh did not understand the meaning of these words at first, he would be familiar soon.

For the two brothers, a journey to the unknown had started. When they were away from their land, they had no news about their family. When they were sailing away, only their stepmother said farewell.

Two days later, they cast anchor close to an island.

Kumma and Semneh followed Nefermaat to a hill with a breathtaking view of the river. In the meantime, two small boats cast nets into the river. Half an hour later, the men started to hit the water with sticks. Kumma and Semneh were watching curiously. When they drew the nets, they were full of fish. Semneh remembered when his father's men were catching the fish with spears. The Egyptians had caught more fish in half an hour than his father's men could in three days. They slept on the island. The next day, they set sail. The beauty of the river was enchanting.

Nefermaat said, "We shall soon come to Abidos. This is a sacred place with the temples and graves of our ancestors. All the pharaohs and their offspring used to visit here."

The ships stopped on the left side of the river. After paying the visits, the prince invited the brothers to his resting place on the slope. While Kumma was walking up to the prince, Semneh stayed on the shore to watch the fish.

Kumma looked back at his brother. He was waving his hands joyfully. Kumma saw a crocodile moving invisibly toward Semneh. He shouted, "Semneh, come here quickly."

Semneh heard the voice but could not understand what it was for. Nefermaat had also seen the beast. He signaled Semneh as well. Semneh saw that they were calling him without being aware of the urgency. He started to walk slowly while the crocodile moved quickly. Kumma took a bow, placed the arrow, and waited. When the crocodile got closer to Semneh and opened his mouth, Kumma's arrow left the bow and hit the tongue of the beast. The crocodile hit its tail so loudly that Semneh saw it and ran away.

Nefermaat and his soldiers praised Kumma loudly. In the Egyptian army, there could not be any man so fast, so brave, or so talented. Semneh had been totally forgotten among. Although Semneh should have felt obliged to Kumma, he felt anger against his brother.

During the rest of the journey, Nefermaat treated Kumma as his best friend. The soldiers who had been a little bit jealous at the beginning were hailing Kumma as their greatest hero. Nefermaat's palace and administrative center of the kingdom were in Memphis.

The prince wanted to surprise his new friends. They tied the boat to the berth in the Garavi Valley. They walked inland, following the water channels toward a lake. The huge reservoir controlled the floods. During the high water seasons, they opened the lids to get the water and fill the pool. In the low water seasons, they used the water for agricultural activities. There were beautiful papyrus and willow trees around the pond. After having breakfast served by the soldiers, they had no other wish except to move to Memphis.

Nefermaat was close to the city. Thousands of people gathered in the harbor. The king and the queen had also taken their seats in their private cabin. The mob was shouting crazily to celebrate the victory of the Egyptian prince. Nefermaat got out of his boat and proceeded to the royal cabin with Kumma and Semneh.

When they came close, he saluted King Snefru and Queen Hetefnes. "His majesty, the king of the upper and lower Nile, the lower Nubian territory and the Allaki Valley is yours."

The pharaoh looked at his son and said, "Your services are the pride of Egypt. I am proud to have a son like you."

Nefermaat said, "Kumma saved my life. If not for Kumma's unbelievable talent with weapons, I would not be here today."

Snefru said, "He who saved the life of my son and his brother are undoubtedly friends of Egypt as well. Welcome to your new country."

The pharaoh was smiling. Kumma thought of his own father. In spite of being the chief of a small tribe, Aspelta never laughed. He thought smiling was a sign of weakness.

The palace was far from Memphis. Kumma would spend the night with Nefermaat. Semneh could not understand where he was. They had followed a long wall. When he saw a large gate with guards in front, he realized they had arrived in a place much larger than their village. When he rose, he saw indigo and turquoise tiles. He stopped to watch.

Since the group was walking, Kumma held his arm and had to drag him. There was a beautiful garden inside. After walking for five minutes, they saw a big pool with tables around it. Kumma and Semneh sat close to the prince. Although the king and queen were supposed to have different seats, Snefru took his son near him. He had a lot of things to say. While drinks were being served to the guests, Prince Rahotep appeared with his wife Nofret and daughter Meresank. He was the chief priest of Heliopolis, a place far from Memphis. They saluted the king and queen and moved to the place reserved for them.

Nefermaat stopped talking to the king to join his brother at the prince's table. He wanted to introduce Kumma and Semneh to his brother. He signaled them to come. Kumma and Semneh stood up and walked toward the table. Nefermaat introduced them to his brother and family members, praising his heroic actions.

Everybody was listening to the prince and watching Kumma carefully. They had been affected by his eagle eyes and powerful figure.

Semneh was standing near Kumma. Once more, he felt a strange anger toward his brother. He was about to regret following Kumma to Egypt until he saw Meresank, Rahotep's daughter. She had not worn a wig as most Egyptian women did. She had combed her reddish hair in a style that shined under the light, spreading a rosy scent. She was watching the new hero admiringly. Suddenly her eyes caught Semneh.

This heated Semneh's blood. Her pink lips and green eyes enchanted the young man. He could have stayed there for a lifetime because he was driven by the colors of love.

6

Love and Art

Semneh and Kumma spent the night in Nefermaat's palace. The sudden changes had made them tired. Semneh still woke up early. He walked out to the garden. There was nobody there except the servants. He followed the road to the pool and saw Prince Rahotep.

Prince Rahotep said, "I heard good things about you and Kumma. How did you find Egypt?"

"There are exciting things and attracting colors in Egypt. We were riding rafts across the river. There are beautiful barks here. We used spears to catch fish. The first time I saw nets was in Egypt. The pond in the Garavi Valley was nice and useful to prevent floods. The most amazing thing for me was your colorful pictures. I have been told that one could remember everything was spoken with these figures. How can it be possible?"

Rahotep was surprised. He was not expecting such clever answers from a Nubian. He had admired Semneh's observations. "Tell me, young man. What would you like to do in Egypt?"

"I do not know. Nobody has ever asked me such a question."

"Would you like to learn the colorful pictures and become a clerk? If you want, you can be trained in Heliopolis. You can even be an artist if you are talented."

Semneh would not dream of being so lucky. Training in Heliopolis meant being with Meresank.

"You have not yet answered, Semneh."

He was so cheerful that could hardly talk. "I have been so happy that I did not know what to say."

Rahotep said, "Then enjoy your luck and be a talented artist."

At the breakfast section, the princes were seated at the same table. Rahotep said, "Kumma, I would like to thank you once more for saving the life of the prince. He told me about your talent with weapons. Would you like to use it to train Egyptian soldiers? Would you always be loyal to Egypt?"

"Oh my great king, it is an honor to have earned your trust in such a short time. What could be more important than this? I can spare my life for you and Egypt—to deserve this trust."

"Kumma, I assign you as the assistant to the prince, but remember. It is not only the soldiers that serve the magnificence of Egypt. If they protect our country against our enemies, artists carry our name and civilization to future generations. Rahotep suggested that I train Kumma in the Heliopolis Temple School as an artist. Semneh agreed. What do you say about it?"

"As much as it is for Semneh, it is also a privilege for me to have an artist in my family. I already knew that his real interest was in art. I noticed how Egyptian civilization had influenced him in the short time we stayed in Memphis. I hope he can become an artist of whom Egypt will be proud and he doesn't disappoint you."

Rahotep would go to Heliopolis with Semneh in the morning.

Kumma embraced Semneh and bid farewell. Rahotep's boat was beautiful, but it could not amaze Semneh anymore. He was used to Egyptian magnificence. Meresank would be on the boat with him. Trying not to be noticed, Semneh was watching the girl. Her hair was lighter. She had a maroon dress and a golden necklace.

Meresank was careless. She was watching the bark. After they were away from the port, the princess turned to Semneh and had the chance to see him. She said, "I learned that you want to be a clerk. Good luck to you."

Semneh thought his heart was dashing. She had addressed him unexpectedly. He said, "From the day I came to Egypt, I liked your colorful pictures on the walls. I hope I will be successful in learning them."

"We call them hieroglyphs. They are our manuscripts."

Semneh was ashamed of his ignorant words, but he wanted to make her talk. "Do you know when we shall be arriving in Heliopolis?"

"We can be there before evening—but don't be in a hurry to get there. Classes are boring, and the lectures are difficult."

Semneh disliked these words because of the impending separation.

The next day, after arriving Heliopolis, class started in the temple school. They gave him a box of paints and brushes. They put a blank papyrus sheet in front of him and wanted him to copy some of the = manuscripts. In this method, the important thing was to be able to copy the figures without knowing the meanings.

Semneh looked at the samples. There were eyes, birds, snakes, and other things, but the most repeated ones were the girls standing and sitting in different positions. All of them reminded him of Meresank. Semneh first tried to draw a girl in a blue gown. He put the arms and legs in brown and her hair in black. The lecturer was amazed. Semneh had drawn almost a perfect figure. The proportion between body and limbs was close to perfect.

The first day, Semneh worked for hours. He had a desire to develop his talents. The hard work continued for days. He was being appreciated by his lecturers—but not by the loved one. A long time passed, but he did not hear anything from his brother or Meresank.

At the boarding school, students used to be put to work when not training. Semneh was left in complete isolation and loneliness. His only remedy was to learn the seven hundred figures of the hieroglyphs. He started painting. He made a lot of friends. He showed great progress in painting and writing. Art made him forget his missing lover.

After lunch, he went to his room, which he shared with his friend Nebet. He started to paint without noticing his friend was close and watching his drawing.

Nebet said, "I have not seen such a beautiful girl in my life. Who is she?"

"She is my dream lover."

"Does it mean she is real or imaginative?"

"You can call her imaginative."

"You were not around since lunch. You mean that you spent so much time imagining her?"

"Can a man without an imagination be an artist, Nebet? In most cases, artistic imaginations are more beautiful than real life. Besides, when I reflect my imagination in my art, I create something real. That is the difference between an ordinary man and an artist."

"You are right, Semneh. You really created beauty. I have never seen green eyes and red, glittering hair."

"You see, Nebet, how my imagination captured your heart. You noticed my dreams were more beautiful than real life. Each artist should exceed reality—in perfection and beauty."

Nebet saw sorrow in the eyes of his friend. They were not the emotions of a creator in these hopeless eyes. "I feel that, in spite of your enthusiasm, you are not happy."

Semneh put his hand on Nebet's shoulder. "You are right, my friend. I feel unhappy when I recollect my past. My mother died when she gave birth to me. I lost my father and young brother in battle. I have not heard from my elder brother in a long time. I feel sorry for the beloved ones I lost."

Nebet said, "You talk in such a tone that it occurs to me that you are in grief. Loss is more than what you recounted to me. Is it possible that you are missing a secret love?"

"You may be correct, Nebet."

"I know this pain, my friend. I once loved the daughter of a priest. It was impossible for me to reach her as a student. When I learned of her marriage to a rich man, I wanted to die. But time is curing the pain. Divert yourself with other lovers—and you will forget."

"What will I do if I cannot forget?"

"Semneh, if a hopeless love elevates your art so much, it is worth of all kinds of pain. If separation inspires immortal works, is it not more valuable than mortal love?"

"I will think all about what you said. I will not forget it. What would you do if you had come across a girl with red glittering hair? Could you divert yourself if you had fallen in love with this girl?"

"You are hopelessly in love, Semneh. I thought you loved an ordinary girl. Don't tell me you are in love with the daughter of a priest or someone who is married to somebody else."

"No. I don't think she is married. If she was the daughter of a priest, I would think of how easy it is to attain her. There is such a big gap between us that I might have a slight chance of reaching her if I become a famous artist. This hope inspires me."

The two friends became lost in their dreams. Their memories had been revived.

Seven months after Semneh started school, he was walking in the temple garden with Nebet. Suddenly they heard the touching sound of an instrument behind the temple. They walked toward the sound. They asked the guard at the gate and learned that it was a new music school.

Semneh was curious. They entered the hall silently. A soft light beam from a window at the opposite side of the hall enlightened a strange instrument with strings. When they came closer, they saw the shadow of two men near the harp. Semneh recognized the voice of Rahotep. He was deeply excited. Could the harpist be Meresank? Finally he saw a glittering red spot. He had no doubt anymore. The harpist was the princess whom he had missed and dreamed of for so many months.

Rahotep noticed Semneh and called him.

Meresank turned and saw Semneh. She stood up to come near him.

Nebet recognized her as the girl in Semneh's drawing. He understood his friend. A man aiming at reaching such beauty could be an artist. He was jealous and pitied his friend.

Rahotep said, "What are you doing, Semneh? I have wanted to talk to you for a long time. It was long ago that we met. You are my guest.

Tell the guards that you will spend the night at my home. There are so many things to talk about."

Nebet wondered how the Egyptian prince could be so friendly with his roommate. He did not have permission to stay near them and left unwillingly. While walking out of the hall, Semneh turned his head and looked at the harp. The love Semneh had lost in the glitter of a colorful civilization had been found by following the magical sound of a harp.

When they came home, Semneh met a lot of young men. He learned that Rahotep had five sons from two wives. His youngest child and the only daughter was seventeen. Meresank was from his last wife, Nofret.

At dinner, Rahotep took Semneh and Meresank on his left side and had Nofret on the other. They finished their meal quickly.

Rahotep said, "My father, King Snefru, stopped the construction of the unfinished pyramid in Meidum and decided to build a new one in Dahshur. Master Imhotep showed him the plan of a new pyramid. When he decided on this, he also wanted to construct a new palace near it. He invited me to help him in the planning process. It took a long time. I had to move to Dahshur temporarily with my family. We had to prepare accommodation for twenty thousand workers and a port for the barks to unload the granite. In the new pyramid, the royal cabin is above the ground for easy communication with the sun deity. It was tiring but challenging work for me."

Semneh said, "It is unbelievable, Prince Rahotep. I would like to see these places."

The prince said, "I also want you to see the construction. Next time I go to Dahshur, I will take you with me."

Semneh said, "If I may dare, I want to ask you a question. You already had a pyramid in Meidum you had been working on for more than ten years. Is it wise to leave it and start a new one?"

Rahotep was expecting this question, but he was not sure the young man would understand the answer. "Pharaohs have to strive for perfection, Semneh. If a more perfect one is planned, the less perfect one can be put aside. It is not wise to delay a perfect job for the completion of an imperfect one. As long as the kings plan for the best, Egypt will be wealthier and stronger. If we can carry our work thousands of years ahead of our time, our civilization will be influential on future generations."

Semneh said, "Prince Rahotep, since I did not hear from you, I have not seen my brother either. That's why I was in so much grief."

"You are right, Semneh. It is a difficult situation, but your brother is in a very good position. He has been successful in training the army. He has been assigned as the chief assistant to Nefermaat. In this post, he is in charge of inspecting the upper and lower Egyptian troops. He has to work hard, especially at the beginning of his mission. I think that's why he could not come to see you."

In the morning, Semneh and Meresank went to the temple with Rahotep. Meresank wanted to continue her music lessons in the temple. Her brothers at home were interfering with her life. Because she was the youngest kid, she had been spoiled. She preferred to take classes instead of being dependent on her brothers. Semneh went to the music class in the morning and sat in a hidden place where nobody could detect him. The lecturer was teaching the students to play simple pieces by memorizing the strings. With repetition, they were learning the difference in the notes. When the class was over, there was a lot of time till evening.

Meresank was pleased when she saw Semneh. "How long have you been here, Semneh?"

"For a long time. I like to listen to the harp, and you were playing quite well."

Meresank started to laugh. "I wish the teacher had the same opinion."

"But you are a beginner now. Do you remember the first time I came to Egypt? I used to call hieroglyphs colorful pictures. Now I am counted among the masters."

"Do you mean I shall soon be a master?"

"I am sure of that. But for today, Meresank, if you are bored of the lessons, would you like to walk along the river with me? I always do it to relax."

"I think that's a good idea."

They found a solitary place with a magnificent view and sat on a rock.

Meresank said, "The pharaoh's palace was too big, and I was alone without any friends. I spent most of my time with the youngest son of my grandpa."

Semneh watched her movements and listened to her voice without much talking. It was about time for sunset. They decided to go back. Meresank slipped on a wet rock. Semneh held her hand and never let it go on the way back. Meresank did not try to pull away till they got very close to the temple.

That night, his friend asked him where he had been. He said he was walking along the riverbank.

The next day, Semneh went to listen to Meresank again. Meresank smiled when she saw him. They decided to go to the same place. When they got away from the temple, Semneh held her hand. They sat together on the same rock. Their daily activities soon became a habit. Their friendship lasted for months. They were having fun talking together and were happy with each other.

One day, Meresank said she was sorry. "My father was sick yesterday. The doctor said he was tired of working on my grandfather's project. He usually feels pain in his chest and is tired. I am afraid of something bad happening to him."

"I am very sorry. Your father is my best friend in Egypt."

"Thank you, Semneh. It's good to know he has a friend like you. If something happens to my father, please don't leave me alone."

"I will never leave you alone, but maybe we are too anxious. Maybe this is an occasional problem."

"I hope you are correct, Semneh."

Meresank put her head on Semneh's shoulder. He was at a loss. His mouth dried in excitement. He wanted this moment to last forever. He thought about what might happen to Rahotep. It could be the end of this friendship. He was sixteen—with no career—and was an alien from Nubia. How could he continue the present situation with her?

But how could he be separated from her? She was his indispensable passion.

In the morning, Semneh woke up early as usual. He was planning his regular meeting with Meresank. He had finished his painting.

His teacher said, "Semneh, you are the most successful student from our temple. You easily passed all your classes. You have proven your talent in painting. I am afraid I don't have much to teach you. I talked to Prince Rahotep about you. If you want, he will assign you as one of the assistant clerks in Memphis. You can be closer to your brother and get paid for it."

Semneh was shocked. He wanted to be close to Meresank—not his brother.

The priest said, "But if you want, you can stay here and study sculpture."

Semneh's burden in his heart lifted. "To be a sculptor is my greatest ambition."

"Then you can stay in the temple and become successful."

Semneh tried not to reveal his feelings. The teacher took him to the master sculptor. He introduced Semneh to him. The sculptor had heard a lot of praise about Semneh. He took him to the working place of the sculpture students. It was an open area with raw stones and hammers.

He gave Semneh a stone block and said, "Listen, Semneh. We shall make a statue out of this stone. What would you like to cut out of it?"

Semneh was excited and said, "I think I would like to make a ram."

"Okay. Take a piece of chalk and draw a ram on the stone."

Semneh paused. He had always drawn two-dimensional figures. His master tolerated his inexperience. He showed Semneh how to imagine three dimensions on a flat surface. He gave Semneh a chisel and hammer. He showed Semneh how to use the hammer. Semneh knew he had to be successful. He threw himself into the work.

After four hours, his master stopped him. Semneh wanted to continue, but the teacher had no tolerance for mistakes.

Before meeting Meresank, Semneh hid so she could not see him.

She looked around and walked outside. Semneh touched her arms from behind. They walked toward the usual place.

"Meresank, you cannot guess what happened today."

"I'm curious. What happened? Tell me quickly."

"The chief priest called me and said there was no more I could learn in writing and painting. He told me that he talked to Prince Rahotep about an assistant clerk position for me in Memphis."

Meresank felt bad. She said, "I congratulate you. When are you leaving?"

"I will stay, Meresank. Would you like me to go?"

Meresank had never been so happy in her life. "Don't tell me you refused the job offer. My father will be angry with this."

"Not exactly. The chief priest suggested I stay in the temple and attend sculpture class."

"Do you mean you are a sculpture student now? When do you start?"

"I have already started. Did you not tell me not to leave you?"

They were quiet for a while.

Semneh noticed how sorry she was when thought he would leave and how happy she was about his refusal. He thought of embracing her but gave up after noticing some priests. Such craziness could be the end of everything. How would Prince Rahotep react to such a new affair?

Semneh thought Meresank was in love with him, but she was tied to her grandfather and the king. The pharaoh would not agree with their union. It was best to wait and work hard to be an artist. That would be the proper time.

If Semneh accepted the offer, he would be close to his brother and make money earlier. He refused it, taking the risk of a new adventure. He wanted to stay in the temple. Meresank knew that the sacrifice could only be made for love. She was not bored when they were together. Was Semneh the hero of her dreams? If their relationship had gotten more serious, what would her father and grandfather say? Meresank realized it was too early to make a decision. She should not have mixed the problems of tomorrow with today's comfort.

Semneh was not close to his old friends. He was in a different class with a different master. He was not too friendly with any of his new colleagues. His days of loneliness were far away. Meresank was by him; who did he need more? His whole world was full of her—and this was more than enough.

One day, Semneh said, "I want to take you to a different place today."

They walked to the open area of the school. Meresank saw a strange object covered by a cloth. The master was waiting for them and smiling. When they came closer, all the students stood.

The master said, "Can you open it, princess? It is the first work of my valuable student."

Meresank could not believe in her eyes. "Can this ram-headed sphinx be made by Semneh?"

"Believe it, princess. This is the first work of Semneh."

Meresank wanted to kiss Semneh, but when she saw the cheers of the students, she controlled herself. She looked at Semneh in such a way that everybody felt there was something more than appreciation.

"Semneh, would you join us for dinner. I'll tell the story to my father."

"Gladly, princess. I want to give my first work to your father as a gift."

The students applauded Semneh. They loaded the statue on a carrying litter. They started to walk to the palace. Meresank, Semneh, master, and students entered the garden and unloaded the statue. In the meantime, Prince Rahotep came near them with some of his family members.

When Meresank saw her father, she pulled away the cloth. "What you see here is the first work of great master Semneh."

Snefru heard about Semneh's achievement. When he came to Heliopolis, he wanted to see the work. The king said, "I congratulate you, Semneh. As the first work of an artist, you achieved the impossible."

After talking to Semneh, he turned to the others.

"People believe that sculptors cut the stones. In fact, they reflect the inspiration of the creative power. This statue is the reflection of the absolute word on stone. It is a conversation between the deities and artists."

Meresank said, "Do you know, Grandpa? Semneh is a successful painter as well."

Snefru looked at his paintings and said, "I did not know you were such a talented painter, Semneh. I will have you decorate my new palace in Dahshur."

The offer could be the greatest reward for others, but it was worse than death for Semneh. It meant separation from Meresank. She was anxious too. No matter how good he was, refusing the king was impossible. Semneh should have found a solution immediately. The fear of losing Meresank made Semneh think quicker.

"I am grateful to your confidence in me, but for a long time, I was planning on making statues of Prince Rahotep and Princess Nofret. If you permit me, may I start your work after I finish theirs?"

"Okay. I approve your suggestion on one condition. After finishing theirs, you will immediately come to Dahshur."

Meresank and Semneh sighed.

The next day, Semneh went to the temple with Rahotep. They explained the situation to his master. He cheered this assignment. He promised to select two stones of the best quality and send them to the palace. The job provided good money for Semneh. Rahotep would pay Semneh in silver.

Meresank said, "Semneh, since you moved here, what would you say if I left school?"

"Meresank, I would be happy to spend most of my time with you, but you recently showed big progress in music. If you leave the class now, you kill all your talent. That's why I suggest you continue your music lessons."

7

Love and Disappointment

Semneh started work the next day. When Meresank was back from the temple, she used to watch him at work, sharing opinions about the statue and talking for hours. Sometimes Rahotep's sons joined them.

Semneh's master from the temple was pleased with the progress.

Five months later, the head of Rahotep was finished. Everybody was satisfied. The most excited person was Nofret. She would be the next one to pose for Semneh.

One afternoon, Semneh was resting under the willow trees. He heard Nofret coming toward him. There was a man with her wearing only a skirt and no shirt. When they came closer, Semneh noticed Kumma. They ran and embraced. So much time had passed since they had been together. Nofret left the brothers alone.

"I could not come to see you, Semneh. After training the soldiers, Nefermaat assigned me as his chief assistant. I saw much of the country."

"Prince Rahotep told me everything. I am proud of you."

"I have heard a lot of good things about you. They say you have been the best student in hieroglyphs, painting, and sculpture."

"What are your plans? Are you going to settle in Memphis?"

"It does not look likely, Semneh. The Egyptian fortresses are under attack on the southwestern border. I shall now control the troops on the frontiers. Maybe Egypt can start a war against Libya."

Semneh asked, "Have you ever been to Nubia?"

"Not yet. When I finish my mission with Libya, I shall go there to find our family."

Semneh remembered his Nubian days. There, he was nobody—and Kumma was hero. Egyptian civilization was elevating the artists to the level of heroes.

Semneh saw Meresank coming toward them. Her red dress made her more attractive than ever. When Semneh stood up, Kumma turned. Meresank blushed at first glance. She knew of his reputation.

Kumma had earned his reputation. Semneh looked like a boy. Kumma felt admiration. He had not known she was so beautiful. For a short time, he stared at her.

Meresank told the brothers to sit. She studied her father's statue and asked Semneh her usual questions. She was not able to withdraw her attention from Kumma. Semneh was aware that she was not listening as usual. He noticed his brother was enchanted by her exceptional beauty. Semneh knew what these glances meant from his own experiences. He felt jealousy and anger. When he remembered his words about leaving soon, he was relieved. A long rally in Libya could take months or years. He would have no time to remember Meresank. He could even die.

Nofret interrupted the silence and said that Prince Rahotep was inviting both brothers to dinner. Kumma sat between Nofret and Rahotep. Semneh was seated near Meresank as usual. Kumma answered Rahotep's questions without looking at Meresank.

The next day, Kumma left Heliopolis. The emotional setback was over for Semneh. Life took its usual course. The statue of Rahotep was about to be completed. Rahotep was very pleased with the result. Semneh was still planning a surprise for him.

One day when the prince was away and not supposed to come back for a few days, Semneh decided to paint the statue. As it was a hieroglyph, he painted the body brown, the hair black, and the dress white. At last, he came to the eyes. He placed white quartz balls in the holes he had engraved for the eyes and pasted black crystals in the middle. The statue had not been more than a stone block before. What was the magic of the colors? Were they the breath of the deities? The statue seemed so alive.

When Rahotep came back, King Snefru was with him. They went to the statue. Semneh and his master bowed before the king and the prince. The pharaoh congratulated both and ordered to start and finish Nofret's statue quickly.

At dinner, everybody was happy. Waiters served drinks after the meal. When Rahotep raised his glass for the first sip, he was hit by a striking pain in his back. His glass slipped away from his hand, and his head fell to the table. Everybody jumped, but it was too late to help him. Rahotep was dead.

The day his statue was finished, his life had been terminated by the deities. Meresank had witnessed the whole process. She ran to her father, embraced him, and started to cry.

Semneh had lost his best friend in Egypt. Nobody could estimate what would happen after this.

Snefru had made up his mind. After the mummification, Rahotep would be placed in *mastaba* (grave house) in Meidum with his statue. The family of his son would temporarily move to his palace in Memphis. He thought he could console the orphans this way. The most urgent thing was the preparation of the grave. Making Nofret's statue was suspended.

Rahotep's coffin was put in a holy boat and was pushed to the port by slaves. Behind the boat, the priests prayed and his sons carried offerings. Semneh and Meresank were watching the ceremony with tears. His body would be taken to Abidos following the course of the sun. The priests would start seventy days of mummification after digging out his organs. In the meantime, Semneh would decorate his sarcophagus.

Semneh was unable to find consoling words for the princess. Besides he was the one who would need most of the consolation. When Rahotep was alive, he had always found an excuse not to be separated from his princess, but he was under the complete command of the pharaoh now. He was scheduled to leave Heliopolis the next day, but they were still too young to hope of coming together one day. It was Semneh's task to please the pharaoh so he could hope to marry Meresank. His artistic enthusiasm found a way out of his pessimism.

Semneh tried to say good-bye to Meresank before going to Abidos. Meresank didn't want to see Semneh before leaving. She could not control herself before the servants. She had cried all night in her room. She was scheduled to leave for Memphis with the family. The king and queen were supposed to go to Abidos to join the prayers. Semneh had completed the decoration, but the mummification continued. He saw the pharaoh's men unexpectedly. King Snefru was calling him immediately.

When he arrived in Dahshur, the palace was completed to accommodate the king. There was a pool in front of the king's lodge. Sculptors were working on lion-headed sphinxes. Part of the water in the pool was flowing through the channels. Far from Snefru's palace, there were houses for high-ranking officers and military guards. Snefru told Semneh what to do. Semneh would decorate the outside wall of the palace with figures of Egyptian beliefs.

Snefru had given sufficient men to Semneh for the project. A month later, the project was presented to Snefru. In the narrow space over the entrance gate, a sun depicted Amon Ra. On the sides of the gate, Osiris and Isis would be drawn. Near Isis, there would be her son Horus and all the deities of the big cities. Near Osiris were his forty-two followers, weighing the evils and goods of the divine balance.

Snefru checked the project thoroughly. Semneh and his assistants worked for more than six months. Two weeks before the completion of the project, Snefru sent Nofret and Meresank back to Heliopolis.

The king saw the decorations and praised Semneh and his men. "What would you like to do after completion?"

Semneh had earned the pharaoh's confidence. He had a strong supporter to permit his marriage to Meresank. His words would be obeyed without objection. "I would like to finish Nofret's statue, which I have not started."

Snefru was pleased. Semneh reminded him of his deceased son.

"Semneh, you are the best friend of my family. Go finish your work."

Semneh could get crazy. In fifteen days, he would embrace Meresank. As soon as he put the last touch on his work, he would go to Heliopolis to start Nofret's statue and propose to Meresank.

Meresank was dreaming in the garden. She woke to the voice of a man. She turned and saw Kumma standing nearby.

Kumma stretched his arms to hold her hands. "I heard your father died and was much grieved."

When Meresank saw the deep sorrow in his eyes, she burst into tears.

Kumma put his arms around her and pulled her head to his shoulder.

Meresank felt his naked chest on her breast. She cried for some time then they sat together.

"I spent my last months at the border. I just learned of the prince's death. I set out as soon as I was aware of that."

"My father was like my friend. After he died, my grandfather took Semneh to Dahshur. I am now very lonely."

Meresank started to cry.

"Don't cry, Meresank. I will never leave you alone, and I share your grief."

"Thank you, Kumma. You display great friendship to me."

Kumma came every day after that and spent his time with Meresank by the pool. They talked for hours. Kumma told her his plans.

"Nefermaat gave me a house near his palace four months ago. I am also alone in the big house. I want to get married and settled in Memphis. If all I plan comes true, I will take Semneh to my house. We live together and will never fall apart. What are your plans, Meresank?"

"Unfortunately I have no plans, no hope, and no tomorrow."

Kumma said, "Will you marry me, Meresank?"

The young girl was amazed and excited. She did not know what to say. Kumma held her hands and looked into her eyes.

"You cannot know how lonely I am. My mother died in my arms when she gave birth to Semneh. By her loss, I was deprived of motherly love. I lost my father and young brother in the Egyptian attack on Nubia. I learned of their death some time ago. I cannot bear this lonely life. I want to have my own family."

Meresank was pleased to find a lonely man who wanted to share her loneliness. She still could not answer Kumma.

"Meresank, I have loved you since the first time we met. Because you were a princess and I was a foreigner, I could not disclose my love, but now I am an Egyptian. I am still doubtful about getting Snefru's consent, but I am ready to take the risk for you since I am not able to live without you."

Meresank was confused. Kumma was a reliable, loveable man. She compared him to Semneh. She did not need to worry about a future with Kumma. She realized her concern about Semneh was a youthful habit. She had good times with Semneh, but would she see him again? Grandfather's mission could take years. She said, "Your proposal makes me happy, Kumma."

The young man sighed. An unknown happiness filled his soul. To think of Meresank as his wife was beyond his dreams. Nothing was real, but he was lucky. Nefermaat and Snefru would visit Heliopolis the following day.

Nefermaat called Kumma when he arrived at the palace. After discussing military matters, Kumma confessed his feelings.

Nefermaat put his hand on his shoulder. "You are the savior of my life and my most trustworthy man in Egypt. Of course I approve of this marriage. I will talk to my father too."

Kumma ran to Meresank and explained Nefermaat's attitude.

Meresank was excited and worried. She was stepping forward to a life that should be experienced by all young girls. Her teenage days with Semneh were coming to an end.

Nefermaat talked to Nofret. In the evening, he discussed the subject with his father. Snefru approved of the marriage because of his appreciation of Semneh. He called the youngsters after dinner and announced their marriage. Everybody was happy, but nobody was aware of Semneh's feeling.

Semneh finished his work in fifteen days. He was in hurry to go to Heliopolis. He arrived at the palace in the evening. He wanted to clean himself. He was going to Meresank's lodge, but a guard stopped him. "The princess married Commander Kumma a week ago and moved to her new house in Memphis."

Semneh was in the greatest shock of his life. He ran to his room to hide his pain. He started to cry. He was talking to himself and asking questions of the deities. After a sleepless night, he pulled himself together. He met Nofret at breakfast.

"Good morning, Nofret. I came here to finish your statue."

Nofret was moved. Her husband's friend had not forgotten her. "How friendly you are, Semneh. Very few people remember the wife of a deceased man. Who can console a widow by making an immortal statue of hers? I was about to leave for Memphis to go to my daughter's house. I will be back in about a month. You can come with me if you want. I am sure the newlyweds will be delighted to see you."

"I don't want to disturb them on their honeymoon. When you come back, I'll start your statue."

Nofret said, "You know everybody looked for you before the marriage. King Snefru praised your art and said he would permit this marriage only because Kumma was the brother of an artist like you."

Semneh had to act cheerful, but he was crying inside. He had nothing to do until Nofret came back. He returned to Dahshur.

When King Snefru saw Semneh, he was surprised and pleased. He could show Semneh his greatest pride—the pyramid in Dahshur.

Semneh was eager to see the pyramid. The next day, they went. Their destination was an hour away on donkeys. Snefru took his youngest son with him. Near the pyramid, Semneh felt small. The pyramid and surrounding details were beyond his imagination. Before coming to the area, they passed through the workers' settlement. Hundreds of cooks were preparing meals for workers.

Snefru said, "We shall use approximately 1.5 million stones in the pyramid. If we place four hundred blocks daily, the construction will take ten years."

Semneh was about to go out of his mind.

Snefru said, "There are twenty thousand men working day and night in shifts. Heavy stones are brought to the pyramid by eight oxen, and a hundred workers slide the stones into the proper places. Unloaded sledges continue from the other side. Once the first row of stones is finished, the ground is elevated by putting more sand and stones on the previous layer."

Semneh said, "I thought pyramids were constructed by slaves through torturing them. I see three times more Egyptians than foreigners."

"Big projects can never be completed without national support."

While everybody was at work, one of the ox drivers shouted at Semneh.

Snefru ordered his guards to bring the man.

Semneh said, "My great king. He is my old friend Idenu and neighbor in my village."

Idenu looked tired.

The king said, "How are you, Idenu? How is it progressing?"

Idenu answered without raising his head. "Everything is progressing as planned, my great king. This pyramid will stand for thousand years as the biggest construction ever made by mankind and will be commemorated with your name."

Snefru liked the answer. "Is there anything you ask from me?"

"My great king, I am not young. My sole wish is to go back my village to die there."

Snefru ordered his guards to set Idenu free. They gave him a donkey and some silver.

Idenu was pleased and paid respect to the king. He thanked Semneh. He put a ring on Semneh's finger; it was the only thing he owned. The king permitted Idenu to come with them till the port.

Idenu whispered, "Semneh, there is a cap on the ring that opens when you press the sides. You will find the poison in it that we used in Elephantine."

Semneh wanted to return the ring, saying that he would not need it. Idenu refused and departed on his donkey.

A month later, Semneh returned to Heliopolis. Nofret was at home. He could start the statue of Nofret. Working hard was curing his heart pain.

Six months later, he was no longer needed for Nofret's modeling. Working alone was his preference. Semneh stood near the stone. He looked at the statue from a distance. He was delaying his work to recollect his memories of the garden. A wind behind him brought a familiar scent to his nose. He turned around.

Meresank wore a pink dress. Her heat burned his blood from head to toe. There were a lot of things Semneh wanted to ask, but he could not find the proper words.

Time had changed a lot of things in Semneh. He was taller, wider, and stronger. He had transformed into a mature artist.

Meresank was aware that she had to break the silence. She put her arm on a tree for support. "My mother's statue looks beautiful, Semneh. I was curious about it. Kumma went away to a military operation against Libya. In order not to suffer from loneliness, I came here."

Semneh put his arm on the statue. He said, "What importance can this have? Did you not enslave me to lifelong loneliness? You were the colors of my life and the inspiration for my art. You were my breathing air, drinking water. I loved you so much. Did you not feel anything for me?"

Meresank's blood was on fire. "I hear your feelings now. Why did you not tell me these before?"

"But did you not know my feelings about you?"

"Maybe I knew, but I needed to hear them. I was aware that you were watching me as an art piece, but my desire was to be touched. You were sharing your days with me, but I wanted to plan my future with you. I wanted to see a brave man confess his love."

Semneh's intention was to blame Meresank, but he felt the guilty. "I would gladly sacrifice my life for you, but I understand my mistake was my desire not to hurt you. I was trying to make up for my shortcomings, but I realize it was a waste of time. I should have followed my instincts freely when I was with you instead of being hindered by my fears. Love and art should be expressed freely without any rules or limitation."

Semneh thought that he had put too much blame on himself. Had Meresank not have any liability in this separation?

He said, "The price of my inexperience should not have been so grave. We were young and had enough time to learn these things. Could you not wait longer?"

Meresank said, "Young girls have two worlds—the real one and the dream world. What I used to share with you was my real world. What I had with Kumma was my dream world. I was a mature woman in this one. Our dreams usually mislead us. We cannot escape from their attractions. While you had no promise for me, Kumma proposed marriage. He knew how difficult it could be, but Kumma dared to do it. Which girl would not hold the strong hand that reached out to her when her father passed away? If a man's love for a woman is not that kind of courage, what else could it be?"

"I dared the most difficult thing in the world to get you, Meresank. I had the courage to be an artist. I created art only to be able to stay longer time with you. When I was in Nubia, I met many brave hunters. They had courage till they caught their prey. Most of them used fake traps to catch the prey and killed them afterward. An artist gives eternal life to his inspiration. I saw the men in Nubia. They were gentle and kind until they got their women. If you held their hands, you would be their slaves. An artist makes himself a slave once he finds a loved one."

Meresank burst into tears before the end of Semneh's speech.

Semneh continued, "Are you happier now than in the days of our togetherness?"

Meresank said, "No, Semneh, unfortunately not. We learn too late not to lose what we had in our hands. When I was with you, I had no future. I was living my days in full satisfaction. I have a future with Kumma now, but my days are empty. Kumma spends most of his time in missions far from me. You were always by me. Unfortunately we cannot go back to the old days."

Semneh said, "Yes, we can. Let us go back to the good old times—even if it is for one day. Let's walk along the river. Let us go to our usual place where we used to watch the temple."

Meresank stopped sobbing and said, "Then let's go back to the old days. Let us imagine we were students—and my father was alive. Even if it's not real, let us pretend to be living in the past. Even if it is a dream, it is worth everything."

Semneh said, "My dear love, if there is an afterlife, why would the same not exist for lovers on earth? If the sun rises after setting in the evening, why should our love not rise again in the horizons of our hearts? If our love survived, why should we let it die now?"

8

Love and Sin

They left the palace and walked along the river. They felt like students again. They came to the place they used to sit. Meresank lifted her legs and supported her back against a tree. Semneh put his arm around her neck and a hand on her leg. While he was fondling her hair, he pushed her close to him and made her sit on his knees. They kept their positions as if they wanted to make up for lost time. They united physically and mentally so nobody would ever come between them. On the way back to the palace, they were silent.

Semneh recalled the richness of his affair with Meresank. He was fond of the color of her eyes. When he was afraid of losing her, he had followed the sound of her music. When he thought his love had turned into ash, the fire of his love was revived by her scent. When he lost his strength, it retuned by touching her skin.

Meresank was ashamed of her sin, but did not regret it. For the first time, she had experienced real love—the love of her youth, her first and the only love. What she lived was worth of all the punishments. If her grandfather had stopped building an imperfect pyramid to build a perfect one, why should she not sacrifice an imperfect love for a perfect one?

They went back home, full of emotions. Semneh was naked and sleepless in his bed. A silent shadow entered his room and came near his bed. When he smelled her scent, he trembled with excitement. He felt her skin on his naked chest. It was the first time the artist had not chased after his inspiration and had instead found her nearby.

With the driving force of his love, Semneh speeded up the making of the statue. In a very short time, a masterpiece was finished. There were no mistakes on Nofret's statue. As it was in love, he had attained excellence in art.

Nefermaat returned from the Libyan operation a week after the completion of Nofret's statue. Egypt had won, and the rebel tribes had been taken under control.

Kumma would come ten days later with the loot and the slaves. It was time to return to Memphis for Meresank.

Semneh had nothing to do in Heliopolis. He went to Nofret and asked her permission to go to Memphis with Meresank. Semneh would accompany her to Memphis and ask for a clerical position from Nefermaat.

Semneh and Meresank arrived in Memphis late in the evening. Kumma had a large house in a garden behind a pool. There was a comfortable guest room and a big bedroom for Kumma and Meresank by the pool.

Meresank prepared a dinner with whatever she could find in the kitchen. Because she had planned a long stay in Heliopolis, she had sent away all the servants. They finished their meals alone. They were uncomfortable and feeling the stormy days ahead. In an anxious mood, they were afraid of talking too much. How long could they continue their relationship?

At that moment, they saw the reflection of the rising full moon on the pool. It highlighted the colors of the flowers, the bending of the branches, and the vibration of the water. This revived their artistic instincts.

Meresank brought her harp and started to play the melody she used to practice in the temple. She pressed her back to Semneh's chest. Her hair was touching on his face, and her scent was infiltrating his soul. Semneh put his arms around her. When she started to sing, he tried to the feel the vibration of her voice.

Meresank was singing a hopeless love song, and Semneh was feeling sorrow in his heart. She stopped singing and turned her face. Her green eyes were full of tears. She was hopeless, like an animal in a trap.

Semneh pressed her head to his chest and started to pet her naked legs and arms, and Meresank fell asleep in his arms.

The next day, they went to Nefermaat. He had missed Meresank so much. The daughter of his deceased brother was another favorite.

Meresank told him about the completion of Nofret's statue and how magnificent it was.

Semneh wanted to stay with his brother and asked if he could find a clerical position for him.

Nefermaat was pleased with Semneh's request. He was searching for a reliable man to control the stock entries and exits. Already seven clerks had been caught in robberies.

Nefermaat called the chief clerk without wasting any time. The clerk taught Semneh everything in two weeks.

Nefermaat was tired after the Libyan operation. He wanted to rest until Kumma came back.

Meresank liked to spend her time with her cousins when Semneh was at work. It was not long before the messengers informed her of the coming of Kumma.

Semneh and Meresank took their seats near Nefermaat's cabin. When the barks appeared on the river, the crowd roared. The first group of soldiers took precautions on the coast. The following barks disembarked with slaves. The loot was carried to warehouses on the port. Because of the early arrival of Nefermaat, the welcoming ceremony had been transformed to Kumma's victory celebration. When the last Egyptian hero appeared on deck, the cries were magnified.

Kumma went to Nefermaat's cabin and bowed. He moved to Meresank and embraced her passionately. He greeted his brother. They were invited to dinner by the prince.

After dinner, Nefermaat said, "Kumma, after the completion of Nofret's statue, I assigned Semneh as the assistant to the chief clerk."

"How can I thank you, Prince Nefermaat? At last, our separate lives have come to an end. The family is reunited."

"Stay with me until you get married. I will not worry about Meresank when I am away on operations."

Glasses were raised numerous times to toast Nefermaat and Kumma. High-ranking officers were telling stories about the courage and heroism of Kumma. Late that night, Kumma was heavily drunk. His men carried him home. Semneh and Meresank followed the group home and fell asleep.

The night was too hot for Semneh to sleep. He walked to the pool. He was irritated by the voices coming from Kumma and Meresank's room.

Kumma said,

"Meresank, my love, why are you running away from me? I missed you so much while I was on my mission."

Meresank said, "I waited for you since early in the morning without resting and we stayed so late at the dinner party. I am still tired."

Kumma was not ready to listen to excuses. "How could it be? We slept long enough to rest. If you still say you are tired, don't move at all. Let me love you as I desire."

"Kumma, let go of my arm—you cause me pain."

"No, Meresank, you are mine. For months, I risked my life for the sake of this night together. Don't you understand how much trouble I had on the Libyan deserts? Why should I wait longer now? Are you not my wife?"

Meresank said, "Please leave me alone. You are hurting me."

Kumma said, "I won't. Nobody can take you away from me."

"I beg you. At least tonight, I need rest."

Meresank's voice gradually faded out. Semneh was furious and had difficulty controlling himself. His princess was suffering. A barbarian act was being committed by his brother. He hated Kumma. He could not meet him anymore. What would he say to Meresank when they met? The poor girl might try to conceal her pain. He damned his own tribal hunting origin. He was a civilized Egyptian rather than a

Nubian. This painful night had given him an opportunity. Civilization was a social order emerging from the fact that men had to be gentler, cleaner, cleverer, and more successful to get the most precious women. In this advanced social order, people liked gentlemen. Rulers aimed at perfection. Nubia, where women were treated as animals to be hunted, could never beat Egypt in art, science, or wealth. If he had met Meresank in Nubia, what would have happened? He would have loved her, but would he have needed to get sculpture lessons? Would he have been an artist? His father could buy Meresank as an asset, but would he have gotten the artistic satisfaction he experienced with Meresank? He thanked the deities for meeting Meresank in Egypt.

In the meantime, Meresank left her bedroom without noticing Semneh. She sat by the pool and started to cry. She was punching her knees and asking why she had married Kumma.

Semneh could not resist. He came slowly to her side and held her shoulders gently.

"You heard everything, didn't you?

"I heard—and hated it. What is he doing now?"

"He is dead drunk," Meresank said.

"I am so sorry and ashamed of my own brother. Do you want me to bring you something to wear, Meresank?"

"It's a good idea. I have a shawl in my room."

Semneh entered the room quietly. He saw the shawl and took it. He was about to leave the room when he saw his brother. Kumma was snoring with saliva running out of his open mouth. On the table near the bed, there was a jug and an empty glass. Semneh hesitated for a moment. He put some water in the glass and pressed the sides of Idenu's ring. He took some powder from the ring and put it in the glass. It was not difficult to pour the water into Kumma's mouth. Semneh washed the glass with some water from the jug and left the room.

He said, "It took some time to find the shawl, but Kumma did not wake up."

After covering her shoulders, he sat near Meresank. They joined hands and stayed silent. Meresank fell asleep in his arms. Semneh was sorry for Meresank, and he regretted his deed. He had interfered with the function of the creative power. He had destroyed what was made by Ka.

"Oh, the creative power who gave life to all living creatures, watching their deeds, listening to their voices. Kumma was my brother. He was always my protector and reasonable to me. He saved my life and opened his house. In return, I killed him—committing a great sin. Can you forgive me? It was not because of his wrongdoings. Because of my jealousy, I killed my brother. I shall draw my most beautiful pictures for you if it will release me from this shame. Let me make the finest statues for you—to make me forget this painful crime. Oh, my great creator. Please don't punish Meresank for my sins. Don't put an end to her life. If you get her in trouble, give me double. I committed a sin because you drove me. If I desired a woman crazily, it is because you inspired me. If you are almighty, you must have the power to forgive."

When Meresank woke up, she wanted to go back to sleep. She entered her room and ran out instantly in fear and panic. She told Semneh that Kumma was motionless.

Semneh ran into the room. He put his hand on Kumma's nose and mouth to control the breathing. He put his head on Kumma's chest and felt his pulse to check the vital symptoms. All had stopped. Meresank was trembling. She recalled that she had cheated on her husband with his brother. In Egypt, many men—including his uncle—would have treated their wives like Kumma. If she had not loved Semneh, she might have given pleasure.

In the morning, Semneh and Meresank went to Nefermaat with tearful eyes. They told him that Kumma was dead drunk when his soldiers brought him home. When they woke up in the morning, they found him passed away. Nefermaat listened to them and consoled them. He was sorry to lose one of his trustworthy men. When Kumma was alive, he was comfortable assigning him to difficult missions.

They decided to put him into a *mastaba* after mummification in the Egyptian traditions since he was a hero. In the morning, his body was placed on the holy boat to be sent to Abidos.

9

Years of Happiness

When Nofret learned the death, she came to Memphis to console her daughter. Nefermaat had given Kumma's house to Meresank.

Nofret decided to leave Heliopolis and settle in Memphis with her daughter. Nefermaat ordered Semneh to move closer to him. Semneh knew that the quicker he gained Nefermaat's appreciation in his new job, the better chance he would have to get Meresank. He worked crazily. He started working first and left last. The chief clerk was satisfied; Semneh had lifted burden from him. In Egypt, levies were being collected in commodities and distributed as such. Semneh was responsible for keeping the records of these movements.

One morning, Meresank was shaken with nausea. She was suffering from vertigo too. Nofret gave her some medicine. Meresank was relieved. She suffered from the symptoms for days. Nofret questioned her and realized she was pregnant. Kumma had died two months earlier, which meant she had conceived on the night of Kumma's arrival.

Nofret and Meresank went to the prince. When they arrived at the palace, Nefermaat was with Semneh. This pleased Nofret. They would learn the good news together. She said, "You cannot estimate how sorry I am about Kumma's death. Your brother was an Egyptian hero and my son-in-law, but now I have some news that will please everybody.

Semneh, you will soon be an uncle. Meresank is pregnant. Kumma's spirit will survive in his child."

Semneh could not know what to say.

Nefermaat said, "Congratulations, Meresank. I hope your baby becomes as brave as Kumma or as cute as you. In both cases, I will do my best to be a fatherly guardian. You can be sure I will display all paternal concern."

Semneh stood up and said, "If you permit me, I would like to take care of Kumma's baby. I could not be sufficiently close to my brother. I want to make it up by always being near his child. You should know that Kumma had foreseen these days. Before going to Libya, he asked me to promise to take care of his family if anything happened to him. If you approve—and Meresank agrees—I want to marry her."

The prince said, "You are going to say the final words, Meresank. I do not want you to grow your baby without a father. It's up to you to make the decision."

"Semneh's words seem reasonable to me; he can really love my baby. Besides, after my husband's death, I do not want to be separated from my mother. I believe Semneh will gladly accept this."

"What do you say about Semneh's proposal, Nofret? Do you approve it?"

"My only wish from now on is to live with my daughter and grandchild. Semneh is the best man with whom I can get along."

Semneh had not dreamed of such happiness. He kept silent.

Nefermaat called the young couple and said, "I declare you husband and wife and wish you lifelong happiness."

Dinner had not been served. Nefermaat ordered his servants to prepare a celebration banquet.

That night, Semneh moved into Meresank's house. Since the house was close to the palace, it would not create a problem. After so much sorrow and death, they had found happiness.

Semneh looked into the eyes of his official wife and said, "From the first day I saw you, I dreamed of this moment. I wish I had come to Heliopolis ten days earlier and not suffered any of these pains.

We can wipe off all our shortcomings now. Let us dream I came just to Heliopolis on time—and I asked for you from your father. It is not too late to revive an immortal love. Will you dare to start everything?"

"I can dare anything with you, Semneh. You proved that artists can be braver than soldiers."

Meresank and Semneh started a new life. They would share art and love as a legally married couple.

Three days after the happy wedding, Semneh woke up while Meresank was sleeping. It was great for Semneh to wake up in the mornings and see Meresank in his bed. Semneh watched his wife. Light beams reflected Meresank's beauty. He silently moved out of bed. He found papyrus, paints, and brushes. He sat and started to draw her. She had turned on her side with one leg stretched forward. One of her arms was below her head. Semneh could not let this moment of exceptional beauty be forgotten, but he could follow the Egyptian drawing rules in which human figures were always shown in profile. With this technique, Semneh knew he could not show any depth. Semneh realized that the anatomic proportions of the human body were being distorted. He noticed that the front sides of the body looked bigger than the other sides. He decided to draw them as he saw them. In half an hour, the sketch of Meresank's posture was drawn.

In the meantime, Meresank was waking up and stretching. When she could not find her husband, she looked around. She saw Semneh drawing something without noticing what was going on. When Semneh focused on the paper, she stood up silently and came near her husband. The drawing seemed alive and real.

"I have watched your drawings for such a long time, but I have never seen such a beautiful one."

"It is nothing compared to your beauty, my darling, but you are right. It is the first time I tried this technique. You always inspire me. Which artist lives with you and does not feel new emotions?"

Meresank remembered her grandfather. When they had informed him of their marriage, he had sent a messenger to invite them to his palace as early as possible. Meresank escaped her husband's arms. "Let's go to my grandfather and take this picture to him."

Semneh accepted the idea. He was dying to show it. "You get ready, my love. I have to work on some details."

Meresank asked Nofret to come with them. She was tired of controlling the servants who were working on changes of the rooms.

When the newlyweds arrived at the palace, the pharaoh was with his architects near a pool in front of his palace. Semneh's drawings on the walls were attracting much attention. When Snefru saw Meresank, he asked his men to leave so he could listen to his granddaughter. Meresank informed him her pregnancy.

Snefru said, "I congratulate both of you once more. I approved of your marriage with all my heart. To grow a baby without a father would not be appropriate. I want you to stay here for at least a month. I missed you very much, and I missed talking to Semneh about art and architect."

The newlyweds liked this offer very much. Meresank would have no household responsibilities, and Semneh would have an opportunity to visit the pyramid.

Snefru saw the stroll in Semneh's arm and asked. "What is that scroll in your arm?"

Meresank said, "Grandpa, Semneh made my picture—and we brought it to you as a gift."

The pharaoh walked to an empty table in the garden. Meresank and Semneh opened the papyrus on the table. Snefru recognized his granddaughter, but he could not understand the three-dimensional picture. "Semneh, till you came to Egypt, our artists have made pictures in two dimensions. You proved that pictures can use three dimensions. You have many talents. We were proud of our ancestors—and just copied them. You have taught us the real merit is in change."

"Oh great Snefru, till I came to Egypt, I could only count ten colors. I have learned the limitless variety of colors. I knew knowledge was being transmitted from father to sons in words. Here I became familiar with hieroglyphs. In my country, soldiers were the most respected people. Here artists are equally respected. Had I not come to Egypt and not met you, how could I be multidimensional and so talented?"

Snefru invited an architect to look at the painting. "Imhotep, I will show you a picture that I cannot understand how it was made. Can you explain this technique?"

"My great king, drawing is my second field of specialty. So let me see it."

The pharaoh and painters gathered around the table. Semneh fixed the sheet on the table and started to watch curiously. Imhotep was not expecting such a complicated question. Other painters were at loss too. The picture looked quite different from what they knew. With no time to study, they could not find an answer.

Snefru felt like a victorious commander. He asked Semneh to explain. Semneh explained the perspective rules he found. Some of the painters had already worked with Semneh. Others knew his reputation. They all congratulated him—with the exception of one. Imhotep was angry because of the humiliation in front of the other painters. He knew he could not do anything to the husband of the king's granddaughter. He preferred to keep silent; in five years, he would finish a pyramid that would not be equaled in thousands of years.

Snefru wanted to show the pyramid to Semneh and Meresank. Khufu, the youngest son of Snefru, joined the group voluntarily. He was seven—and had been born at the same time as the pyramid. He had watched all phases of construction.

Meresank and Semneh were amazed by the progress of the pyramid. They congratulated Imhotep.

While they were drinking their beverages, Snefru found Semneh looking at the pyramid carefully. He had closed four fingers, raised his thumb toward the pyramid, and closed one of his eyes.

Snefru asked, "What are you doing, Semneh?"

Semneh turned to the guests and architects. "It is an incredible thing, but there is a deviation between the right and left angles of the pyramid."

"There cannot be such a thing," cried Imhotep.

Semneh wanted to close the discussion and said, "I am afraid I was wrong."

Khufu said, "Show me what you did, Semneh."

While Semneh was explaining, most of the guests could not see any difference.

Khufu said, "Semneh is right, Father."

After that day, Khufu would always love and respect Semneh.

Imhotep's hate for Semneh multiplied. He had humiliated him near so many people. It was his idea to start a pyramid in Dahshur before completing the one in Meidum. He had convinced Snefru of the importance of making a bigger one. A Nubian had caused suspicion in the mind of the king and gained the trust of the young prince. If there had not been sand platforms around the pyramid, he would measure it precisely—but it was impossible to do this. "My great king, such a deviation cannot be proven now. When the pyramid is completed, no proof will be needed."

Everybody was relieved, including the king. After returning to the palace, Khufu never left Semneh. He often asked questions and tried to learn as much as possible. Snefru was happy about Khufu's interest in Semneh.

Meresank and Semneh asked the king to go back their homes. Khufu did not want them to leave. They could hardly convince him and promised to come back soon.

The newlyweds were unimaginably happy. Nofret loved Semneh like he was her own son. She was proud of his success in his new job. Nefermaat had seen Semneh's work at the Dahshur palace and congratulated him.

Before Meresank gave birth, the pains started. Semneh was worried since his mother had died in childbirth. When the doctor came to Meresank, he was out of his mind. He recalled the night he poisoned his brother. He started to cry regretfully. "Oh, creative power. Have you forgiven me or just waited to punish me by taking Meresank or my child away from me? If I was the one who committed the sin, I must be punished. If children pay for the sins of their fathers and women suffer for the wrongdoings of the husbands, where is your justice and absolute power?"

When noises came from the room, he heard his name. They were calling him. He ran to the room. Nofret told him it was a girl. When he saw Meresank in bed with the baby, he felt all the blessing and forgiveness of the creator. He had spared the lives of Meresank and the baby.

The baby stopped crying when he took her in his arms. At that moment, a stream of compassion flew from his heart to his baby. He looked at Meresank admiringly. She had created a human. She was the representative of the deities. She was a mother, the most esteemed of all personalities.

Meresank loved watching Semneh. The baby might not be from him—but he had never hinted this. "I love you, darling, and am very happy now."

They gave the name of Semneh's mother to the baby—Nitokris.

10

Farewell to Earthly Life

Three happy years after the birth of Nitokris, Semneh was playing with his daughter in the garden. The little girl was so fond of her father. In her all naughtiness, she was trying to find refuge in her father's arms and wanted to share her toys with Semneh. Nofret was in her best days. Snefru liked his youngest granddaughter. Nitokris was Khufu's favorite playmate. Nefermaat had organized a birthday party for her favorite niece and invited the family.

Five days before the party, guests started to arrive. For the party, they gathered around a table in the garden. Snefru opened the ceremony and called the little girl. Nitokris sat on the knees of her grandfather and put her arms around him. This demonstration of love pleased Snefru. He gave her a golden necklace with lapis gems.

The queen put a bracelet from the same set on her arm. Nitokris liked the presents very much. She was petting each of the stones. Other guests lined up to offer presents in front of the king.

Nitokris thanked all of them.

When they got home, Meresank embraced her husband and said, "I am very happy with you, Semneh. It's like a rebirth every day."

Semneh woke up early and walked into the garden. When he heard screams from Nefermaat's palace, he rushed to the palace. The guard at the gate told him the prince had died. Semneh staggered. He had lost two close friends in Egypt.

While walking, he saw Snefru. "I killed them, Semneh. I loaded the whole burden of construction on them. Is a pyramid worth two sons?"

Semneh had difficulty finding words of consolation for King Snerfu. Life had to go on. Snefru went back his palace and focused on construction.

One morning, he saw some stones rolling down. It was followed by a terrible uproar. The pyramid had slipped to the side—just as Semneh had warned. His disappointment was beyond definition. So many years of work had been wasted. He called the architects. Imhotep suggested that construction would help avoid the anger of the king. Snefru asked them to investigate and prepare a report. He decided to go to Memphis to talk to Semneh.

After Nefermaat's death, his elder son took over. He welcomed Snefru and listened to him in sorrow.

Snefru was not in a mood to hear words of consolation. He ordered Semneh to come. He said, "You had noticed the inclination first, Semneh. I do not trust anybody but you. I want you to come and live in Dahshur with your family and be my assistant."

Semneh did not like Snefru's situation. He could die as suddenly as his sons had. He agreed immediately. Snefru cheered. He believed that there could be no mistakes when Semneh was around.

When Semneh explained his conversation to Meresank and Nofret, they agreed to move to Dahshur. The king and Semneh went to see the architect report.

When they arrived in Dahshur, a nice surprise excited the family. The king allocated a big house for them and three servants. They had no difficulty adapting to their new life. Everybody loved and respected them.

The queen was enjoying her talk with Meresank. Nitokris was the favorite playmate of Khufu. Semneh did not need to work long hours as the chief consultant of the king. Meresank had more time to spare for her daughter. The architects submitted their report to king. It seemed that the corridor could not stand the weight of the stones. Under the circumstances, it was impossible to carry the king's coffin to the final resting chamber.

Snefru was in shock. So many years of hard work had been wasted. Semneh said, "I want to see the entrance corridor on the plan."

Snefru said, "Semneh, can you find a solution to this hopeless situation?"

Imhotep opened the sketch. The corridor was going at ground level for about forty steps, leading to an intermediary chamber for adaptation of the afterlife. According to the new belief, the pharaohs were supposed to ascend to meet the deities. A second chamber for this meeting was above ground level. Demolition had blocked the entrance to the first chamber.

Semneh said, "Since the corridor collapsed, we can open another corridor to the intermediary chamber. If the chamber is not damaged, the problem is solved."

The architects jumped on this idea and agreed. Snefru approved the plan. "Do what Semneh suggested."

The king sat in his chair. The architects left him alone.

Khufu sat on his father's lap. "Don't worry, Father. Semneh can find a solution."

"Can you really do it, Semneh?"

"Great Snefru, I owe my happiness to you and your sons. If it helped, I would sacrifice myself, but nobody can help you except yourself."

"I have been the king for more than twenty years. I wanted to leave monuments to endure for thousands of years, but I could not complete any of them. I grew old and lost two sons. And worst, I lost my hope. How can I help myself? Obviously the deities don't want me to be recalled as a great king."

"Rahotep told me that the primary duty of the pharaohs was to search for perfection. If they could not find it, they would at least set an example for their children. If we believe in tomorrows, our children will definitely complete what we could not accomplish. Maybe the deities put all these difficulties before you because they wanted you to be remembered as a great king. Let us start the construction of a third pyramid in the meantime renovate the first two. No other king completed three pyramids in his lifetime."

"Do you suggest I start a third pyramid? This is impossible."

"No it is not—just contrary to logic. We suspended the work in Dahshur temporarily. It is a great opportunity. Instead of leaving our men idle, we look for a new site where the ground is solid. We can test until we find a place like a granite mine. In the meantime, we try new construction methods to solidify the building. We can even do more. The steps of the Step Pyramid in Medium city can be flattened to change its unpopular shape. If we use our time cleverly, we can do it all."

"Let's do what Semneh suggested. If you cannot finish, I will do it and give it your name."

Snefru embraced Semneh and said, "Thank you, Semneh. You revived my hopes, which I had lost. Can you tell me where and how you gained this wisdom?"

"My great king, I earned this wisdom in Egypt. You decided to build an unmatched monument. I aimed at an unmatched love. Pyramids can stand the test of time. Great loves are recalled in minds timelessly. No matter how many times I lost Meresank, I have been courageous and tried again. You can achieve anything if you keep up your courage."

Snefru implemented Semneh's plan. The new construction site was found on the north of Dahshur. A new sketch was drawn. Since that area was rich in iron ore, it would be called Red Pyramid. The stones would be vertical instead of the conventional horizontal system. This would reduce the construction time and strengthen the monument. Semneh suggested a shorter corridor to the intermediary chamber to reduce the load of the stones, but it posed another difficulty. Because the final chamber was above the ground level, there would be a steeper passage to move the coffin up to the chamber of final rest. Semneh suggested solving it with a stair system to avoid another demolition. Snefru studied the new sketch. Everything looked all right, but it was not as high as he had dreamed. Semneh thought it would be done by

Khufu. While a new corridor opened in Dahshur, the Step Pyramid was flattened.

Another year passed. Snefru was no more hopeless. Bad news came shortly. The intermediary room collapsed. According to Snefru, fifteen years of work had been wasted. Semneh had a different opinion. Demolition had made the use of the burial chamber impossible. Otherwise, the monumental pyramid would survive for thousands of years. Snefru did not want to think of what would have happened if he had not taken Semneh's advice into account. He ordered a new Dahshur pyramid. He was not spending more time to control the construction. That was Semneh's job.

The next ten years were the best times in Snefru's life. Finally, the Red Pyramid was finished as the third one. The Step Pyramid had been turned to a real conic form. Egypt had gained dominance against Nubia and Libya and become the wealthiest country. New construction techniques were found. The first king of the fourth dynasty would be known for his monuments, his humbleness, and his determination.

Semneh was also in the happiest days of his life with his wife, daughter, and Nofret. He was also the most respected and trusted man of Khufu. To surpass his father, Khufu was counting on Semneh. Nitokris was happy in her grandfather's palace. She was an accomplished painter in Egypt. The limitless gardens of the palace were her main source of inspiration. She was looking at the water lilies by the pool. She was fond of beauty. She had just turned fifteen and was a charming girl.

She fixed papyrus paper on the table to draw the flowers carefully. She started to paint them. She was so artistic that the flowers became animated. She watched her work from a distance and admired herself like Narcissus. She had focused on her painting so much that she did not realize Khufu was standing behind her.

"Beautiful, Nitokris."

She turned back and almost collided with the prince. "You scared me, Khufu."

Khufu was twenty years old. As the only candidate for the throne after the death of his elder brothers, he was the favorite of the Egyptian girls. In spite of the attention of the others, he was secretly in love with Nitokris. He could not disclose this because they had lived as sister and brother for many years. Semneh and Meresank were like his virtual parents. Meresank took care of their needs. Semneh had to answer their questions, but they were not children anymore.

Khufu had been patient with his feelings, but now he was out of control.

Nitokris asked. "Do you find my painting beautiful?"

"I did not look at it."

"Then what did you find beautiful?"

"You, Nitokris. I find you more beautiful than anything else."

A warm wave captured her body, and her faced blushed visibly. It was the first time Khufu had talked this way.

Khufu was faltering emotionally. He was relieved and did not want to miss his opportunity. "Will you marry me, Nitokris?" The young girl did not know what to say, but Khufu was not in the mood to listen to any objections. "You will marry me, Nitokris."

Nitokris said, "Okay. If you want it so much, we will marry."

Khufu was about to go mad. He held her tightly to make up for so many years of passion.

The news spread very quickly. Nobody had felt anything before. Not long after the event, everybody was joyful. Snefru was the happiest one since he knew the reluctance of his son and the need for a wise man to advise him. Semneh was the best person for this role.

The Egyptians knew Nitokris was a talented painter and liked their future queen. In Egypt, queens were assistants to the Pharaohs. It was important to have a favorite woman in that role.

Two months after the royal marriage, Snefru got sick and could not be saved. Khufu and Semneh were with him for his last moments. He smiled and said he was very happy.

Semneh was filled with sympathy. The old man was at peace before passing away. He thanked Semneh for his happiness.

Seventy days of mourning were announced. Citizens were crying about their beloved king who had given them thirty glorious years.

While the coffin was shipped to Abidos by boat, Khufu and Nitokris took the same road. The takeover ceremony of the kingdom would happen in Abidos. Semneh was busy. He would decorate the coffin during mummification. He would meet the architects to set up the device to carry the coffin to the final resting chamber.

Semneh finished his work ten days before the mummification. There was no problem moving Snefru to the intermediary chamber along the straightway. The problem was elevating it to the final resting chamber. Semneh suggested pulling it up with ropes on lubricated wooden slipways. The architects agreed. The problem was that if those pulling from above loosened the ropes, the coffin would fall and break.

Semneh suggested doing it in small steps and filling the bottom with rocks to break the fall. This was a burdensome—but safe—way. Short delays were not of any importance.

When Snefru's coffin arrived in Dahshur, it was easily moved to the intermediary chamber. To elevate it, they implemented Semneh's plan. They realized it was not an easy task. The stones would stop a fall, but the workers upstairs could not hold the ropes until the stones were placed at the bottom. In the middle of the upper chamber, the coffin would be placed in a sarcophagus.

Semneh told the workers to turn the ropes around a solid block each time they pulled. This action helped in spite of the occasional slip. There was still a synchronization problem between the workers at the top and the bottom. Semneh went up to the final resting chamber to help them. At last, they succeeded. Everybody was happy and tired. They sat near the sarcophagus. They heard a whistle like a snake or running water. Semneh looked down and understood everything. The corridor was being filled with sand. It was a precaution against theft and was supposed to be operational after they left the chamber. They had been trapped and buried alive.

Semneh explained everything to the workers. He told them he would not die in great misery and would poison himself. The other workers asked Semneh to end their lives in the same way. They placed the coffin in the sarcophagus and drank the poison. Semneh was the last one to drink. Before taking the glass in his hand, he recalled Elephantine. It had been Idenu's idea, but had he not poured the poison into the pot. When he had poisoned his brother, there was nobody else around. He had committed this sin because of jealousy. He had begged for Meresank's life. He drank the poison and regretted being a sinner.

When Semneh woke up in the realm of divine light, he recalled his earthly experience. He was a Great Angel. He deeply regretted being prayed to as a human. He could not be a good supplicant in the world. He had committed an evil sin. His punishment would be the eternal extinction of his soul. That was what he thought would match his sin. He wanted to have another opportunity to be forgiven. He soon perceived the divine appeal:

> *Punishment and forgiveness for no one to interfere,*
> *Balance of evil and good humans can never confer.*
> *In the world of illusions, you may look like a sinner.*
> *In the stage of evolution, you've been a great winner.*
> *Your beautiful love was an inspiration for your art.*
> *Your sins have all been excused for the sake of a remorseful heart.*
> *All the works you have accomplished reflect divine beauty.*
> *All your deeds are certain steps on the way to eternity.*
> *You will suffer for your sins in a way of quite rough*
> *You'll never be left alone for a minute and a half.*

Part II

11

The Story of Putting into Extinction

At the end of the eleventh century, the Roman Church initiated series of changes after the election of Urbanus II. The first task was to reconcile the relationship with Eastern Christianity because they were under the threat of Muslim Turks. Seljuks, in a short time, had captured a great part of Anatolia and knocked on the doors of Western Christianity.

Pope Urbanus invited the representatives of the Byzantine Empire's Alexius to the council he organized in Piacenza in March 1095. Alexius took this invitation as an opportunity and sent his men to the council. Urbanus gave the floor to them. Representatives of Constantinople explained that the Turks were about to terminate Eastern Christianity and the next turn would be the Roman Church. Muslims had become stronger and wealthier since the seventh century. They had occupied southern territories in central Asia, marched in China and India, and from northern Africa to Spain. If the Turks had continued their march, nobody would like to imagine the future.

Pope Urbanus started a long journey that year in France. He was calling all Christians to the November meeting in Clermont. He went to Valence and Le Puy in August, Avignon and St. Gilles in September, and Lyon, Burgundy, Cluny, and Souvigny in October. The Council of Clermont would start on November 18, and the pope would address them on November 27. Europeans were excited to listen to the pope. Thousands of Christians gathered in the cathedral square. The papal throne had been brought for the speech.

After sanctifying the crowd, he said, "My dear Christians, holy lands where the Son of God was born, are under occupation. Muslims rule in Jerusalem. It is impossible for us to visit the sacred places there. Under these circumstances, if we do not fulfill our duty as confirmed believers, how can we expect to save our souls? You should know that the primary duty of each Christian is to end Muslim dominance on holy lands. I appeal to all of you. It is the time to join our forces to found a great army. I tell you that no one could stand against this army because it will be a Crusade. I tell you that those who take part in this Crusade will be forgiven for all sins."

The call mobilized many people, and there were two groups among them. The first group, the noblesse, was clever enough not to attempt any adventure before being fully prepared. The second group was composed of fanatic adventurers and dreamers. French monk Pierre Hermit was among them. He took the roads to visit many countries in Europe. According to him, the operation would be very easy with the support of Jesus Christ. He was hurrying to start before the nobles to collect the most loot. The task was so easy—and the promises were so attractive—that he quickly gathered an army of beggars and thieves without any military experience.

On April 19, 1096, Pierre Hermit and his friend Roland Legrand were watching their followers from a high hill in Cologne. Roland was the son of Pierre's neighbor in Amiens. His father was a priest in the church, and his mother was the daughter of a rich Armenian farmer. Pierre became a monk, and Roland preferred to work in his mother's farm. In those years, peasants in Northern Europe were in danger. Barbarian attacks and lootings had deprived them of all their belongings. Nobles were safe behind the walls of their fortresses and not very interested in the problems of the poor. Worse, Europe's heavy floods in 1094 brought a shortage of food and deadly plagues. All of this misery created a favorable environment for people to join the Crusade.

Pierre said, "How many soldiers you think we have collected so far?"

Roland answered, "Additions to our group continue. My rough estimate is we should be around twenty-five thousand now. In the meantime, the Germans are gathering under the command of Gottschalk and Leisingen."

Pierre said, "This is bad news. The majority of our group is French. If we wait longer, the Germans may outnumber us. We may have to be under their command, which will not please any of us."

Pierre opened the map of Europe. "Which way do you think is better for us?"

Roland looked at the map and said, "According to my knowledge, the army gathered by the kings will follow the southern route from the Adriatic to Byzantium. Under these circumstances, it will be better for us to follow the northern route from Danube to Constantinople through the Hungarian kingdom."

"You are right, Roland. If we follow the same route as the kings, we may slow down." Pierre looked down to the ocean of tents. "There is only one problem. The Germans might have thought of the same way."

Roland said, "You are right. I am skeptical about their early marching. We have to act quickly without the notice of anybody."

Pierre said, "We move tomorrow, Roland. Lots of Christians may join us on the way."

Roland liked the idea.

They implemented the plan and went down to visit the tents. Everybody was excited. At last, they would reach the Eastern treasures. On April 20, the French Crusaders set out along the Rheine. They arrived at the Danube after Neckar. People were welcoming the Crusaders cheerfully everywhere and offering everything they possessed.

They needed a long rest and camped in Semlin, Hungary, but problems arose shortly. The Crusaders could hardly buy their needs from the citizens. The Hungarians were reluctant to do business with the Crusaders because they did not like to bargain. On Saturdays, there was a marketplace in the main square.

One of the strong leaders of the Crusaders, Geoffrey Burel, was in the market with his men. He wanted to buy a pair of boots. "Vendor, what is the price of those boots?"

The shoe vendor pretended not to hear Burel.

"Are you deaf, man? I asked you the price of the boots."

The vendor was quiet.

Burel held his arm and showed him the boots. "I want to buy these boots. Understood?"

The vendor was a tall, strong man. He pushed Burel to the ground. One of his men helped him up. While walking toward the vendor, Burel pulled out his long sword.

The vendor realized the seriousness of the situation and wanted to run away, but some Crusaders blocked his way. He felt the sword stab his back and fell in a lake of blood. The Hungarians in the market were terrified. Some ran to their homes; others attacked the Crusaders with whatever they could find. They injured some of the French soldiers, but the weapons of the Crusaders were superior. A few minutes later, there were only dead bodies in the marketplace. Shouts and screams were heard in the camping area.

Pierre and Roland woke up and rushed to the marketplace. When they came, they were too late.

Burel said, "My colleagues, the people of Semlin had not paid proper respect to us. We should give them such a lecture that everybody will understand the strength of the Crusaders. Semlin is yours. All precious materials in the homes and women are also yours—on the condition that you don't leave any tracks behind.

Pierre shouted, "Cannot be. Let's pick up the animals and food. Why do we kill the people?"

Burel said, "We can find precious loot in the homes."

Pierre said, "But those people are Christians. There could be women and children in the homes. What threat can they be?"

Burel said, "If we leave any living soul behind, they can inform the Hungarian king who will send his troops to kill all of us."

Pierre said, "At least don't touch the little babies. They cannot talk."

Burel said, "If they lose their parents, they cannot survive and will die in pain."

When the conversation was over, the Crusaders attacked. They were breaking down doors, raping women, looting, and killing everybody. The followers of the pope planning to save the Christians—were killing them instead. Pierre was regretful, but he was unable to stop anything. In two hours, four thousand Hungarians had been murdered.

At the beginning of September, the Crusaders arrived in Constantinople. News from Semlin preceded them. The emperor did not let them into the city, but he provided them with supplies and guides who led them to the Asian side of the city. They were alone in Anatolia. They marched toward Nicaea, which was the capital city of the Seljuk Turks.

Sultan Kilicarslan was on the eastern border of his country. He immediately changed his route when he heard that the Crusaders had set foot in Anatolia. Hermit's group arrived in a village that had been occupied by the Turks, but most of the citizens were still Orthodox Christians. On the Seljuk-Byzantium border, these incidents were common, but there was an unwritten agreement between the parties that conflicts would not affect the native people. The Crusaders were not aware of this agreement. They attacked when they saw minarets in the village. The Orthodox citizens ran into the church and tolled the bells to proclaim their identities. The Turkish commander waited for the Crusaders, hoping to talk them, but it did not happen as expected. While the first row attacked, the others ran into the houses. Screams of the raped women and murdered men echoed in their ears.

While being raped, a mother shouted, "Maria, take your sister and run away."

The girl grabbed her six-month-old sister and said, "We are Christians. Please have mercy on us."

A horseman came close to her; with one swing of the sword, he chopped off her head. Maria was still holding her sister.

Pierre could not bear the tragedy and closed his eyes.

Roland moved quickly and took the baby in one arm. He dragged his friend into the church with the other arm.

Many Orthodox Christians were praying. When they heard the baby cry, they turned in excitement. Roland and Hermit went to the priest. They kneeled in front of Mary's statue.

The priest told his assistant to take care of the baby. He looked at Pierre with red eyes. Although he did not talk, he had many questions. The same questions were in Pierre's mind. Burel and his men had seen Hermit and Roland enter the church, but they did not dare to follow.

The people who found refuge in church lived. That night, the people dined together in the church. Everybody found a place to sleep. Nobody dared to leave.

Hristo invited Hermit and Roland to his bedroom; there were three couches.

Hristo asked, "Do you want something, Brother Hermit?"

"We thank you very much for your hospitality. I cannot tell you how sorry I was; the incidents were beyond my control."

It was impossible to console Hristo after that. "We, as Christ said, loved our enemy Turks and lived in harmony. You are killing your own brethren using Christ's name. Jesus revived dead men and fed five thousand people with five loaves of bread. You are murdering and looting the bread of five thousand for five of you. God spoke about sowing the infertile land and harvesting it a hundredfold. You are sowing the seeds of hatred and cursing fertile land. You did not come to fight for Christianity. You came to destroy Byzantium for the sake of looting."

Hristo's words affected Roland and Pierre. They could not find anything to say or any reason to object. The arrow had left the bow. They realized that the targets were their own brothers and sisters. It was too late to turn back.

The next day, the soldiers informed them that they were leaving. Pierre and Roland left the Crusaders and found an excuse to proceed to Constantinople. It was the right moment. The Crusaders turned to the coastline to sell their loot but were trapped by Sultan Kilicarslan on the way. Most of them were killed—just as they had murdered innocent people.

The noblemen who planned to join the Crusade were not dreamers like Hermit and his followers. They passed the winter in preparation. In 1097, an army of six hundred thousand was composed of the best knights of Europe. After the cold winter days, they proceeded to Byzantium from different corners of Europe.

During that time, Roland and the emperor had become friendly.

The first group to arrive in Byzantium was Bohemond of the Normans. The next day, they were accepted by the emperor. Comnenus introduced Roland as one of his best men. Bohemond had a good impression of both men. Soon, other groups arrived at the city. The emperor was leading the armies to the Asian side and talking to the leaders of each army. He promised them all kinds of support, supplies, and guidance in return for their agreement to return the occupied Byzantium territories. Until setting out, the Crusaders waited for papal instruction about who would be the commander of the army. When they formed a joint commanding committee, the first target was Nicaea. The Crusaders could not occupy Nicaea, and the sultan was not in the city. He was on the shore of a lake. The city had strong walls and fortress.

On May 21, Roland woke to bitter shouts. Sultan Kilicarslan had attacked the Crusaders on the sides of Raymond and Le Puy. Most of them were sleepy and tried to protect themselves with whatever they could find. In each confrontation, some were falling down and screaming while others were continuing the fight.

Bohemond preferred to watch from a distance. Robert de Flanders was the first to help Raymond attack the Turks from the right. Bohemond ordered an attack on the Turks from the left. The Turks were squeezed on three sides. They soon retreated and disappeared.

After the fight, Bohemond and Roland checked the casualties. There were many dead bodies and injured soldiers. Some had been cured.

"Roland, my friend, please save me. My arm is terribly aching."

Roland turned in the direction of the voice and recognized the owner. "Gerard, is it you?"

The injured man was his friend from his village. He had asked him to join the Crusade. His right arm was cut off, and his left shoulder had been broken. His arm was still bleeding. "Please help me, Roland. I am dying."

Roland took off his shirt and tied up the arm. Bohemond told one of his men to find a stretcher to carry Gerard. Roland took his head in his arm gave him some water. "Don't worry. I stopped the bleeding."

"You said it would be easy, Roland. Jesus would help us."

"Don't lose your faith. Both you and Jerusalem will be saved."

"I believe nobody—not you or the pope. I realize how our deeds were against the teachings of Jesus. I killed four in Semlin? While I was raping a woman, I was trying to steal her bracelet. When I had difficulty pulling off the bracelet, I cut off her wrist. I see now how she felt."

Gerard could not speak more and died.

The Crusaders lost 15 percent of their soldiers. It was difficult to occupy Nicaea under these conditions. The soldiers were in need of rest. The Turks in the fortress had watched the battle but were not impacted. The Crusaders decided to discourage them.

The head of the Turks had died on the battlefield; they put him on their spears and paraded him in front of the castle. The Turks were motionless. They asked for help from Emperor Comnenus. It was an opportunity to prove that the Crusaders would not be successful without the help of the emperor. He sent his ships to the castle and set the citizens of Nicaea free. He put his soldiers in the city to open the gates. In the morning, the Crusaders were surprised to find no Turks in the city.

Roland was unable to find a proper answer to the recent incidents. He did not know who was an enemy or who was a friend? If the Turks were the enemies, why did Comnenus free them before handing Nicaea over the Crusaders? If the Byzantines were friends, why had the Crusaders killed them? If the Christians were brethren, what was the meaning of massacre in Semlin?

It was obvious that Anatolia had melted different races and religions in the same pot over thousands of years. The Crusaders had been undesired aliens in this land. The next day, they would move, but nobody knew what the future held for them. They were defeating armies with no glory.

The Byzantine guides had told them that the road to Dorylaion (Eskishehir) was full of deep valleys and steep cliffs. It would be risky to move the whole army on the same route. They decided to split the forces, and Bohemond was on the front line. When they arrived in Dorylaion, they forgot all their troubles. The river cooled the weather on the hottest summer days. They decided to set up camp and wait for the second group of Crusaders. There were plenty of fruit trees along the river. The soldiers jumped in the river to swim. They picked delicious apples, peaches, and plums from the trees. Everybody was happy; nobody recalled the difficult days. Forgetting was the main antidote for their troubles.

Roland woke up early to the songs of the birds. Bohemond was walking among the soldiers. Bohemond did not want to be caught by surprise. From the hills behind the camping area, the Turks attacked. The sultan noticed the split in the Crusaders and gathered his army in a short time. Bohemond tried to check out the attack with his limited forces, but the Turks were progressing. Roland hid behind an old pine tree.

In a short time, the two armies met. The savagery, screams, and cruelty began again. Those who would respect each other in normal life were stabbing fallen soldiers and beheading the injured. Inhumanity used to be called heroism in the battlefield.

Roland did not follow Pierre. Bohemond woke him up from his bitter thoughts. He gave him two men and three horses and asked him to inform the other group. They came to help and changed the fate of the battle in favor of the Crusaders. The river was flowing with blood. Mankind had polluted nature—and their souls.

The Crusaders were uneasy with continuing the Turkish attacks. The Byzantine guides suggested taking the southern routes to escape. The commanding committee decided to turn south in July. They reached halfway to Konya without any problems. A week later, they found diminishing plants and water. The few wells along the way had been filled with stones. They managed to rest during the day and proceed at night, but none of them had enough strength to take more steps. The commanding committee gathered without much hope.

Bohemond said, "If we are exhausted from hunger and thirst and so close to our next destination, then we slaughter our weak horses, drink their blood, and eat their meat."

The commanding committee members initially rejected the idea. When they thought further, they found no other way. Bohemond's proposal gave them enough strength to reach Konya.

When they arrived in Caesarion (Kayseri) on September 10, it was getting cold. They wanted to move as quickly as possible on the way to Marasion (Marash). They stopped before a mountain. A narrow footpath encircled a hill, but they reached the peak without any problem.

Roland stopped on the way to watch the beautiful Marasion Plain. Once they were down, they would have no problems at all. They started to descend joyfully. The footpath was narrower and full of cliffs. Roland felt a raindrop on his face. He had sweated while climbing and was pleased by the cooler weather and rain. The rain increased its intensity, creating floods on the slope with mud, stones, and branches. One big branch hit the legs of two horses. They fell on with a soldier who was trying to stop them.

The bitter scream of the falling man froze their blood. They were shocked by the shouts of two other soldiers who had slipped down the cliff in the intensified rain. Everybody sat wherever they were, trying to hold something. All these actions were useless against the flowing streams. Countless men fell until the rain slowed.

In October, they arrived in Antioch. The city was under Seljuk administration, and the commander was a Turk called Yagi Siyan. When he saw the Crusaders, he realized he could not stand any longer against them. He sent messengers to other Muslim states for help. Antioch was still not an easy bite. Twelve-kilometer walls from the mountains to the Asi River had been fortified by 360 towers. The Crusaders took their positions, and the siege began.

On December 30, Bohemond invited Roland to dinner. "We had

a lot of trouble, but we are in Antioch. We shall celebrate the new year here. What an incredible story, isn't it?"

"It is because of you. If you had not suggested drinking the blood of our animals and solving our hunger and thirst, none of us would be living today."

"Do you think they will appreciate it?"

"The Crusade taught us a lot. We learned how ugly mankind can be behind the mask of religious consideration. We learned that we had all kinds of evil in our souls—killing, stealing, lying, cruelty, and ungratefulness."

"You are right, Roland. We should not expect much from them. I wonder if we shall succeed in capturing Jerusalem. Will these troubles be rewarded by the Lord?"

As Roland was about to answer Bohemond, the ground started to quake. Bohemond held Roland's arm. It was adding up. A table in the middle slipped to the corner. Arms fell down, and some were broken. Most of the Crusaders did not know about earthquakes. They ran out of the tent and staggered.

Roland said, "It's earthquake. Leave your tents immediately."

He dragged the count outside. It was raining heavily. Some of the soldiers preferred to stay in the tents. The masts on some tents broke. Heavy winds drove the tents. Some painful screams were heard inside the tents. Roland and Bohemond used a tree as a shield. The animals were more terrified than the soldiers were. They were running away crazily. The earthquake demolished most of the tents. The soldiers had to stay outside all night in the rain and freezing cold.

In the morning, they realized that some of their friends were injured or dead. They were hungry and had no food. They used their animals as food, but it only lasted a few days.

The food shortages grew in winter with no hope for help. The noblemen of Europe adopted the lifestyle of their prehistoric ancestors and managed to survive by hunting cats, dogs, mice, and rabbits on the farms and gathering fruits and leaves. While they were determining what to do, they learned that a Muslim support group was on its way.

They defeated the rescue army before becoming completely exhausted. The committee met, and Bohemond took the floor.

"My colleagues, we have survived till now with great difficulty. We heard that an army of Genoese and British troops will be here in two days to help us. If we can get the help, we'll have spring before us with warm weather—and no rains, earthquakes, or food shortages. The next two days will determine the fate of the Crusade. Those days will not only be of vital importance for us—but for Christianity as well. Two days will change the balance between Islam and Christianity. That's why I suggest standing for two more days."

"You speak well, Bohemond, but you don't tell us what to do about food."

Bohemond looked at the suspicious faces of the committee members. "No, Duke de Bouillon, our food did not run out. Conditions are grave, but we still have some food." All the men looked at Bohemond with unconvinced eyes. "You know we recently defeated a Muslim army. If we eat the flesh of the enslaved soldiers, we can surely stand two more days."

The committee members listened to Bohemond; after some consideration, they realized they had no choice but to accept the extreme alternative. They managed to survive until the support army arrived.

Spring brought warm weather. They built a tower to stop any help from outside and provided security. They failed in capturing Antioch. Roland was happy. He was walking the hills in warm days. He climbed a higher peak and saw a man watching the Crusaders. There was nobody near him. They saw each other and started to talk after saluting. He was an Armenian, born in Antioch. When the Turks took the city from Byzantium in 1084, they did not touch the citizens. He had attracted the attention of Yagi Siyan shortly after the occupation. He converted into Islam and changed his name to Firuz. Roland became a friend of Firuz and regularly met him on the hill.

The Crusaders learned that the ruler of Mousul, Kerboga, was on his way with an army of four hundred thousand to break the siege of the Crusaders in Antioch. That was meant to end their operation.

One night when Bohemond was walking in his tent, Roland was with him.

"Our situation is grave, Roland. We cannot beat Kerboga's forces. Our adventure will terminate in front of Antioch. In addition to all our efforts being wasted, I am afraid the Turks will be encouraged after our failure to start a counterattack on the Europeans."

"My dear count, I have an idea, but I don't know if it could be useful."

"Tell me quick. We've got to try everything."

"I was walking on the hills some time ago. I met a man of Armenian origin called Firuz. He told me he was an entrusted man of Yagi Siyan."

"This is our last chance. You can save all of us. Tell Firuz that he will be readmitted to Christianity and will be given a fortune."

The next day, Firuz was waiting on the hill.

"Firuz, I learned confidentially that a huge papal army was on its way to end this operation and capture Antioch."

"I heard Kerboga was on his way to help the Turks."

"Kerboga changed his mind and is now in front of Edessa (Urfa)."

Firuz looked disappointed. "That is bad news. It means our time is running short."

"I am mostly worried about you, Firuz. The Crusaders are very cruel men. You cannot believe what they did to the Christians in Semlin and Nicaea. They raped, looted, and killed everybody."

"I am an original Christian. Do you think they will harm me?"

"That is what I am trying to tell you, Firuz. These men are on a Crusade, but they have nothing to do with Christianity. In Semlin, the people were Christians, but no one could escape."

"I am afraid, Roland. Can you help me?"

"If you want the truth, your meeting me is a great chance. I am one of the favorite men of the emperor and the count. I can save you and make you the owner of a fortune."

"Thank you, but how much can I trust Bohemond? What if he gives up?"

"You are absolutely right, Firuz. If the count does not sign the paper, I will not be in the deal anyway, but if you are suspicious about Bohemond, how can he trust you? I shall bring you a written document. What guarantee do you offer in return?"

"I shall bring you my son as a guarantee."

The next day, both men were excited. Firuz brought his son. Roland gave the paper signed by Bohemond. He had offered a fortune in addition to the admittance to Christianity.

Firuz said, "These twin towers are under my control. On June 3, I will hang rope ladders to let the Crusaders in."

Roland went to the count with Firuz's son.

Bohemond called the committee to meeting. "Kerboga surrendered Edessa for three weeks. He gave up and turned to Antioch. We have now three options before us. We can run away and save our souls or stay and die together."

"What is the third option, Count Bohemond?"

"I will let you in without any fight."

"Can you do it, Count Bohemond?"

"Yes, Count Raymond. This is possible if we act quickly."

"How will you do this?"

"I have a man inside the walls. He will let us in."

"But this is dishonesty—an act not proper for Crusaders."

"Is that so? Don't you remember we killed Christians in Semlin and Nicaea? Was this an honorable act? Do you want to die honorably and forget Jerusalem, Duke de Bouillon?"

Duke Robert said, "No real Christian can forget Jerusalem. I fully support Bohemond. Is there anything else you want from us, Count Bohemond?"

"I have saved your lives. I have paved the way to Jerusalem. History books will not mention the failure of the Crusaders. In return, I want Antioch from you."

"We promised the emperor we would return his territory."

"Correct, Duke de Bouillon. In return, he said he would assist us in Anatolia. As a matter of fact, that is what Comnenus did for us. We were short on water on the way to Konya. We were dying from hunger in front of Antioch. Can anybody say we received good support from the emperor?"

Nobody could answer. They had no choice but to accept Bohemond's proposal. They took the oath to give Antioch to Bohemond.

Firuz hung down the rope ladders on June 3. The Crusaders climbed and opened the gates. The soldiers attacked the houses in the early morning. In the eagerness for loot, they were killing everybody indiscriminately.

Firuz had not thought the civilized noblemen could be so cruel. Suddenly, he recalled his sister and mother. He rushed to his house, but he was too late. Firuz was shocked. He had betrayed those who trusted him—and he had gotten divine punishment right away.

12

Rebirth in the World

The captures of Antioch and Jerusalem were welcomed in Europe. The cities were among the most important centers of Christianity. St. Peter's Church was made by digging out the Staurin Mountain; it is considered the first temple of Christianity. One of the Bible writers, Matthew, lived there and wrote about the life of Jesus.

Antioch was the fifth center of Christianity after Rome, Alexandria, Jerusalem, and Constantinople. After the foundation of Antioch, the city returned to its Roman roots.

Bohemond assigned a place for them to trade. They turned the city to an important commercial center for the Mediterranean and provided an intersection for the trade routes from East to West. The fertility of the Amik Plain was based on agriculture.

Roland easily forgot his painful days. He enjoyed the moderate climate, fertile landscape, and developed trade with Italian businessmen. He married the daughter of a rich Genoese merchant and became very rich. He had one son and two daughters. They married the noble members of the principality, but he still served the Church. He trained his children with family traditions. His successors grew up with tales of the Crusades.

It was a sunny summer day in 1252. Citizens in Antioch celebrated St. Paul on June 29. Sheep and newborn lambs were out to pasture.

Even on the outskirts of Silpius Mountain, the plants were in bloom. It was the first year with Bohemond VI on the throne. Father Roland Legrand was trying to fix the details properly.

Bohemond entered the church, knelt before Mary's statue, and prayed. He sat in the first row. The chorus started to recite the hymns. When it was time for the sermon, Roland was ready to talk. A messenger came and informed him of the birth of his first child. Prince Bohemond wanted to be the godfather. The girl was named Angelique.

Thus, the Great Angel was born a second time. Roland was the happiest man in the world. She was his first child; since her godfather was Bohemond, her future was guaranteed. The beautiful baby had blue eyes and blonde hair; Roland foresaw his family as in-laws with the members of the principality.

13

After Fifteen Years

On June 28, 1267, Angelique saw her father in the garden. Roland said, "Good morning, Angelique. Why did you wake up early today?"

Angelique pointed to the servants cleaning up the garden. "It was too noisy outside. I could not sleep and wanted to see the preparations."

Roland looked at his daughter. She was the most beautiful girl in Antioch. Her hair glittered in the sunshine. "Tomorrow will be a very important day for us, Angelique. Prince Bohemond will introduce his new governor to the public in our church."

"You know who he is, Father?"

Roland had learned all the details from his friends in the palace. "Governor Simon Mansel is a relative of the prince. He came from France."

Angelique wondered if he was handsome. "Has he brought his wife?"

"Our new governor is young and single."

The people gathered in front of the church before nine o'clock. They were anxious to see the proceedings of the noblesse and high-ranking officers of the principality. After the guests entered the church, there was thunderous applause.

When Prince Bohemond and his family arrived, the assistants of the chief priest moved to the gate. Prince Bohemond was leading the group. Angelique saw a tall man behind them. The attendants stood up to greet the prince. The chief priest invited the new governor inside.

While he was walking, Angelique noticed how handsome he was. He looked kind and gentle. Angelique was bewitched by the governor.

The chief priest blessed Mansel with water. The audience applauded the new governor unwillingly. The people were against any assignation outside of Antioch. Mansel took the oath with the guidance of the priest and put his right hand on the Bible. He was about to move to the floor to deliver his speech when he saw Angelique. He stopped, suddenly forgetting the speech. When he regained control, he said, "Dear Antioch citizens. I cordially thank the prince and princess for choosing me as the governor of Antioch. Although I am new here, I love this place very much—the weather, nature and people. You are nice, kind, gentle people. If you have a problem, wish, or suggestion, come to me. If we join hands and hearts, we can easily carry this heavenly place to a brighter future. Don't forget, from now on, I am an Antioch citizen as much as you are."

The audience applauded the governor wholeheartedly. The governor looked at Angelique and went back to his seat.

The chief priest started a long sermon with tales from the Bible. The governor did not hear anything. He was not interested in anything but Angelique. He asked the princess sitting near him if she knew that young lady.

"Angelique is the daughter of Roland."

At the end of the service, the prince and princess left the church with the new governor. Angelique tried to forget her sweet dreams. It was useless. A governor from a noble family would not have anything to do with an ordinary girl like herself.

Angelique would not need to wait long to realize her mistake. Three days later, she was at the breakfast table with her father and mother.

Roland turned his wife and said, "You know, darling, we received an invitation from Bohemond to a reception in the court to celebrate the coming of the new governor."

Mrs. Legrand was not expecting this. She said, "Oh my god. I have to prepare a nice dress quickly."

"No, Helen. You need to prepare two dresses. Angelique will come with us. She was invited personally by the governor."

The young girl was excited. Helen was surprised. How did the new governor know the name of her daughter?

They worked all week long. Helen prepared a red dress for Angelique and a dark blue one for herself.

When they were about to leave, two guards entered the garden. They bowed in front of Roland.

"Prince Bohemond sent his coach to take you and your family to the palace."

Roland could not believe it. Sending the court coach to transport a guest was a very privileged treatment. The prince used to ask Angelique along each time he met Roland, but he had never displayed such a gesture. The coach easily took them to the palace, which was located between the internal and external walls near the Asi River. Guards led them to the gate. A pathway in the garden led to a square in front of the palace.

Angelique was bewitched with excitement about meeting the governor. The tables were in the square—a big one for nobles and several for the guests. The young governor welcomed each guest and showed them their seats. Angelique had not noticed how long she walked. She found herself in front of the governor and blushed. It was the first time she had seen him so closely.

"I am very glad that you could come, Miss Legrand."

Mansel turned his hazel eyes to Angelique. He gave Angelique and her family the closest seats to the nobles' table and turned to the other guests. Angelique watched the guests but could not find a familiar face.

After all the guests were seated, horns were blown. All the guests stood up. The prince and princess had arrived. Bohemond delivered a short speech to start the dinner.

Toward the end of the meal, a guard came near Angelique. "Prince Bohemond waits for you at his table, Miss Legrand."

Angelique looked at her father to ask for his approval. Roland nodded.

When she arrived at the table, Simon, the governor stood and gave his seat to her.

Prince Bohemond said, "Angelique, my daughter, how beautiful you are. I called you to introduce Simon." He turned toward the governor. "Simon, Angelique is my baptized daughter. She is the granddaughter of the Legrand family who saved us from defeat against Kerboga and helped capture Antioch."

Simon smiled at Angelique. "I am pleased to meet the granddaughter of such an important family. Can I see you again?"

Angelique said, "If you want to see me, you can come to the church, Governor Mansel."

Angelique and her family went home near morning. She was tired, but she could not sleep for a long time. The new governor was extremely handsome. Had she found the prince of her dreams? The governor had personally invited her. He had smiled and looked into her eyes. He had asked to meet her again. Could all these marks be evidence of his interest against her?

For a week after the reception, she heard nothing from the governor. Angelique missed him and didn't talk much. She could not ask why the governor did not appear. "Good morning, Father. Where are you going?"

"Prince Bohemond called me. I am going to the court."

She was glad her father was visiting the palace. At last, she could get some information from her father.

That night, at the dinner table, he said, "The prince took me to the city walls today. He ordered the governor to repair some of the worn points. He was working at the head of the workers."

Angelique was relieved. She could not rejoice long because her father announced his next decision.

"I have decided to go to our summer resort in Seleucia Pieria next week."

If the flame of love had not been sparked in her heart, she would be very glad. Seleucia Pieria was a port of Antioch. The family had a mansion where they used to spend the hot summer days. Angelique's would be miserable away from the governor. In her absence, another girl might steal young man's heart. She said, "Can we visit St. Peter's Church before we go?"

Roland was not skeptical. St. Peter's Church was a sacred place, and he visited frequently. It was just above the Antioch walls. For many years, Angelique had amused herself by hiding in the rock tunnels and worrying her family.

Her mother said, "I also want to visit St. Peter before the journey."

Two guards would escort them to the church. The horses for Helen and Angelique were ready. They set out in the morning. It was not a long distance, but they had to climb a hill. At Silpius Mountain, Angelique could see the wall repairs. The soldiers noticed Angelique and told the governor.

When the governor noticed Angelique, he rode his horse over to her. He got out of his horse to help Angelique and her mother. They walked to the shade of the old pine trees.

"What great happiness to see you here."

"We came to visit St. Peter's Church."

"I know it's a shame, but I have not visited this church."

"Would you like to visit with us?" asked Angelique.

"Of course," Simon said.

After visiting the church, Simon sat between them. "I have wanted to visit you for a long time, but my work here was too urgent. Baybars, the king of the Mamluks, is an aggressive man. We should always be ready."

Mrs. Legrand asked, "Does he pose a threat to us—coming from Egypt?"

"If he is an ambitious man, he can, Mrs. Legrand. When the Crusaders captured Antioch, they covered a longer distance."

"Next week, we are moving to our summer resort in Seleucia Pieria. Which place is safer do you think?" Mrs. Legrand asked.

The young man did not want to scare them. "If we are strong, everywhere is safe. You can go to your resort safely, but we shall miss you."

"Why don't you visit us when you finish your work here?"

A week later, Angelique was finishing her breakfast and watching the sea from the garden. When a small boat appeared, Angelique said, "Look, Mother. Vahram comes."

The son of the gardener was two years older than Angelique. They had grown up together. Vahram had later become a fisherman. He could find fish when nobody else could. He took Angelique and her father sometimes, and they had great fun.

Vahram tried to pull his boat onto the sandy beach. When he straigthened, he was holding two big fish. He walked over to Angelique and her mother, left the fish in front of them, and bowed. "I pay my regards, Mrs. Legrand. How are you, Angelique?"

"This must be your lucky day, Vahram."

A week later, Mrs. Legrand called Vahram and said, "The governor of Antioch will visit us tomorrow, Vahram. You will please me if you go fishing tomorrow and catch some red sea breams."

The young man went out to his secret places early in the morning. After catching four fish, he sailed to Legrand's house. He saw a crowd in the garden. He pulled out his boat and walked to the garden.

Mrs. Legrand said, "Here, my dear governor. Our fisherman has proven his talent."

When Simon saw the fish, he could not hide his amazement. "Congratulations, Vahram. I have never seen such big sea breams."

Vahram put four fish in front of the governor. Mrs. Legrand rewarded Vahram generously. In the meantime, he looked at the governor. He had never seen such a handsome, gentle man. His heart filled with jealousy. He had no chance of competing with this man. His only hope was if the governor already had a sweetheart. Angelique struck his attention. She was laughing loudly near the governor. Vahram wondered why life was so cruel for poor people.

The full moon lit the dinner table in the garden. Roland Legrand and the governor sat at the heads; Mrs. Legrand and Angelique were on one side. The port master and the governor's escort were on the other side. While they tasted Cappadocian wine, the cook brought the grilled fish.

"I have never eaten such delicious fish."

Mrs. Legrand said, "In order to find this taste, the fish must be fresh and cooked properly."

"How long do you plan to stay in Seleucia Pieria?" asked Angelique.

"After I control the border troops, I'll come back and stay a few more days."

"You will always be welcome in our house."

Roland's words were supported by all family members. After the dinner, the port master and escort left. Helen asked to be excused because of a headache. Roland followed her.

When Angelique and the governor were alone in the garden, he said, "This place is heaven. I'd like to spend my life here—if I were not the governor."

"Why don't you stay longer?"

"I have to control our troops on duty. I shall try to stay longer when I return."

"But then the moonlight will not be so beautiful."

The young man held her hands. "The greatest beauty of this place is you, Angelique. Can anyone, after seeing the glitter of your golden hair, notice the silver of the moon? If you were by me, what other light would I need? Angelique, I have loved you from the first moment I saw you in the church. I looked for chances to be with you, but I had to serve Prince Bohemond and Antioch. I always thought of you when I was not with you. You were always in my dreams when you were away from me."

Angelique could not have dreamed of such happiness. "I was very impressed with your speech and behavior, governor. I did not forget your personal invitation."

"Angelique, don't call me that—at least when we were alone. That's how lovers do."

The young girl did not answer; she only nodded.

Simon said, "Angelique, will you walk to the shore with me?"

They walked through the garden, holding hands. The moon illuminated the sea, the sand, and the beach.

Angelique started to skip stones as she had as a child. "Can you do it Simon?" She found a flat stone and tried again. "I skipped it six times? Come on, try once."

Simon liked the game, but he was not successful at the beginning.

"You failed again, Simon. Watch how I do it."

Simon did it after several more failures. "Okay, Angelique. Let's race."

Angelique took off her shoes and started to run in the warm water.

Simon tried to catch her. Their laughter echoed on the shore.

"Angelique, let's have a rest. May I help you put on your shoes?"

Without waiting for an answer, he kneeled in front of her. He cleaned her sandy feet and dried them with his handkerchief. After putting on her shoes, he put his head on her lap. He put his arms around her belly. They were trembling in excitement. "Angelique, I love you so much that I am scared of losing you."

"I love you too, Simon. Who can separate such great lovers?"

Simon did not want to make her sorry. "I want to share your dreams and never let the happiness in your eyes fade."

Simon stayed two more days. The two days transported them to a dream world. When it was time to depart, he said, "Angelique, I have to leave today. It's worse than death to leave you even for short time, but I will try to be back as quickly as possible. From now on, I have only one goal in life—to spend my life with you. I want to marry you when we are back in Antioch. Do you want to share the rest of your life with me?"

"That is the best question ever, Simon. To carry your family name is the most precious gift to me. I would not exchange your love for the most valuable treasures in the world."

All week, Angelique felt the sorrow of loneliness and the joy of hope.

When the servants came to inform her of the governor's arrival, she ran to the garden gate.

Simon jumped down from his horse, and they rushed to embrace.

"I greet you with all my respects, Miss Legrand."

"Welcome, Governor Mansel."

Mrs. Legrand ordered the servants to lead the governor to his room. When Simon came back, he said,

"I found a lot of shortfalls in my inspection. Our troops are not ready for an attack. News from Egypt confirms that Baybars is about to prepare a great army. I am unable to stay longer. I have to rush back to Antioch to inform Bohemond. I leave tomorrow."

Angelique's happiness faded when Simon went his bedroom. She waited at the garden to see him again, but her dreams did not come true. When she woke up in the morning, Simon had already left.

The Legrand family normally stayed in the mansion till November, but they turned back in September. Angelique was missing Simon and was angry at him for having left without informing her. Was he lying about spending the rest of his life with her?

A guard entered the garden and said, "Are you Miss Legrand?"

"Yes, I am."

"Governor Mansel asked if you can come to St. Peter's Church tomorrow."

"Tell him I will."

"Thank you, Miss Legrand." The messenger left quickly.

Angelique's heart was beating. She could dream again. She was sleepless all night and left early in the morning to meet Simon at the church.

"Angelique, you cannot know how much I missed you."

"Why did you leave Seleucia Pieria without informing me? You could have bid me farewell."

"You think it would be easy for me. I thought about seeing you several times, but each time I gave up. I knew I would never be able to leave Seleucia Pieria if I had seen you."

"But you have not visited me either."

"I could not because Prince Bohemond was always out in case we were attacked. He went to Byzantium two times in one month and left me to represent him."

"Is our situation so grave?"

"If Prince Bohemond had not established good relations with our neighbors and convinced them of the magnitude of the threat, it could be. At least we are not alone now."

"What about us, Simon? Shall we see each other once in a quarter?"

Simon halted for a moment. He had asked the same question several times. He said, "Angelique, you are my most desired ambition in life. There has been nothing more important than you after I met you."

"Why don't we marry right away then? I don't want to live apart from you."

"Angelique, you make me happy and proud, but I love you so much that I have to put your security before my happiness. If Antioch is occupied, being known as Mrs. Mansel would be a serious risk."

"Simon, why don't we marry and go to a safer place—your country, for instance."

"What about your mother, father, and those who would not be able to run away? You are the granddaughter of man who made the conquest of Antioch possible for the Crusaders. How can you think of leaving?"

"How did my family make it possible? It was because of the massacre of innocent people and the help of a traitor. Such dishonesty should not be a source of pride for any of us. The pope who started the Crusade never knew the fear of humans under siege. He never felt the pain of those whose heads were chopped off. I feel their fears. I live with their hopelessness. I don't want to share the same pain. I won't accept the dishonesty of my family by sacrificing my love."

Simon took Angelique in his arms and held her tightly. She was crying. "Angelique, from now on, nothing is important for me but you—not my governorship or what they say about me if I run away with you. Your words have taught me unheard truths. Your love has showed me undisclosed realities."

"Then prove it, Simon. Let us run away from this accursed place before the fires of hell cover us. Let's reach the heaven of our love."

"I shall immediately try to get in touch with the Genoese merchants to find a ship to take us to Europe. Let us keep it a secret between us."

From that day on, they met frequently. Each time, Simon sent his men to the church to tell Angelique their meeting place. The last time they met in St. Peter's Church, Simon was excited. "At last the expected news has come, Angelique. A man promised to take us on his ship as soon as the stormy season is over."

Angelique said, "That means we shall soon have a home where our children can grow up safely."

"Yes, darling. We shall live our heaven in the world without any fear. It will all happen because of you. You showed the correct way to my heart—and to my mind. We shall have Christmas in three weeks. Let's get married and finish our secret meetings."

Angelique was happy but became serious. "You have not yet proposed to me."

Simon held her arms and kneeled in front of her.

"I love you so much, Miss. Legrand. Will you marry me?"

Angelique said, "I love you too, Mr. Mansel, but you must ask my father."

"Let's go to your home then. I shall ask your father."

"But it came too quickly. I should have informed my father about your visit."

"No, my darling. It is not quick; it's late. When a man meets a girl like you—if he found the love of his life—he should move before anybody else does."

"But you should have known that—no matter how late you were—I would wait for you."

"Even if I knew it, I do not want to lose any time with you as a couple. I know how precious the times we've lost are."

Angelique and Simon found Mr. and Mrs. Legrand in the garden.

Simon said, "Mr. Legrand, I loved your daughter at first sight. I want to marry her with your permission."

"Dear governor, your proposal honors us—and we gladly accept."

They were married in Bohemond's palace two days before Christmas.

March was beautiful in Antioch with the scent of the blooming orange trees, the bleating lambs on the green meadows, and the rising waters of the Asi River. In the spring of 1268, its citizens were deprived of enjoying these beauties because of the threat of the Mamluks. They had captured castles in Yafa and Beaufort. The next target was Antioch because of its wealth. Some citizens were trying to strengthen windows and gates and hiding their valuables. Under Silpius Mountain, tunnels led out of the city. Some people were reserving proper hiding points in the tunnels.

In the morning, Simon said, "Everything is ready, my darling. In three days, a Genoese ship will be sailing with us."

Angelique was worried about what she would say to her parents. "That's good, Simon, but what will we say?"

"I shall say I want to examine the troops one last time. You can say you want to pick up your personal belongings before any possible looting."

At dinner, Angelique said, "Father, Simon will go to Seleucia Pieria tomorrow for a last check of the troops. I want to join him to pick up some of my belongings against possible sacking. I just wanted to inform you."

"Be careful, my girl. Those places can be dangerous. Don't leave home—or Simon."

"Thank you. I shall do what you say. I will not leave home. Don't be worried if I am delayed."

"We will not worry, Angelique, when you are with Simon. Don't worry about us either. Men cannot escape destiny."

Her father's words hurt Angelique. Had he spoken deliberately or incidentally? She felt the pain of leaving her parents when they were in danger. Could she save them? "Won't you come with me?"

"It is not worth it to go for such a short time. You go for us. We may not see it again."

Angelique embraced her parents as if they would never see each other again.

Simon woke up early. He had provided a coach for her comfort. After loading their belongings, they set out. Simon stayed close to his wife in the coach.

Angelique was looking at the places that she would not see again and recording the details in her mind. "I passed through these roads countless times. This is the first time I realized how nice they were."

"I know how you feel. Although I have been here for a short time, I thought I was in heaven when I first came. I realize that heaven was in our minds and hearts. If we are happy and safe, we feel good. I know that if Baybars takes Antioch, he can easily turn these places into hell. If we save ourselves, we can at least keep it in our memories."

As they went farther, Angelique's pain lessened. His words had relieved her mind, if not her heart.

"If the Mamluks capture Antioch, there will be no trace of my country. My only consolation is my belief in our eternal love."

"Yes, my darling, our love will survive forever—and worth all the sacrifices."

When they arrived at the summer resort, Simon was enchanted by the scent of flowers. The cook met them at the gate. The other servants had left a long time ago, but the Surpik family lived there while they were gone. Angelique saw Vahram and the gardener on the pathway. They dined together. They had learned of Angelique's marriage and congratulated her.

Angelique said, "Vahram, will you take us fishing tomorrow?"

Simon said, "I was born in central France and have never caught a fish."

Vahram answered without looking up. "Of course I will, if the governor orders me to, but you must wake up very early."

"Don't worry, Vahram. We shall be ready whenever you wish."

Angelique and Simon were tired and went to bed early. They woke up at the same time. Surpik had prepared a rich breakfast for them. She gave them food and water in a basket for emergencies at sea. It was still dark. The boat was big enough to take three of them. In the middle of the boat, there was a seat to take the oars and a sail yard in front.

Vahram said, "Let's push the boat together. You two hold the left. I will push from the right." When the boat was in the water, Vahram said, "Angelique, you take the front seat. The governor can take the rear."

Vahram helped Simon and Angelique take their seats. Vahram pushed it farther and jumped in. He took the oars and sat near Simon to steer the boat. A strong wind started to push the boat.

Simon said, "I never thought that sailing was so relaxing. Nothing is visible ahead, but you steer the boat. Is there a risk of hitting a rock?"

"Not if you know the waters. We have to move in the darkness because we have about an hour to our destination. We should be there before sunrise for a good catch."

Simon was enchanted by the scent of the seaweed. He was unable to keep his eyes away from the phosphorescence on the water.

Vahram said, "Would you like to steer the boat, Governor?"

"If you teach and warn me, I would love to."

Vahram put Simon's hand on the rudder and left.

"I can't believe it, Angelique. I am steering the boat."

"You steer like an old captain. Beware of the rocks."

"Don't worry. Everything is under the control."

"We are getting closer to our destination. You can take over on the return if you'd like."

Simon left the steering to Vahram. He led the boat to a small bay and cast the anchor. He furled the sail. He gave the rear seat to Simon, taking the middle seat. This was necessary to prevent tangling of the lines and gave enough space for Vahram to help both sides.

He put the fresh bait on the hooks and said, "We have to be patient now. If your line is pulled strongly, tell me."

After a long time, Angelique caught one. Vahram quietly left his line, took a scoop in his hand, and waited for the fish to be brought out of the water.

Angelique said, "Watch me carefully, Simon. If the fish swims up, your line will be lighter. You should pull it out quickly, but if the fish swims down, your line will be stretched and you should loosen the line so it doesn't break."

After ten minutes, they saw a big shadow in the water. The animal was so tired that it was floating near the boat without any movement.

Vahram dipped the scoop into the water, took the head into the net, and raised it. It was a red sea bream—at least ten pounds. Vahram caught two more fish before the biting stopped. Nobody was talking; they were afraid of spoiling the magic. Nobody wanted to awaken to the realities of the ugly world.

Screams from the seagulls broke the silence. A bright beam rose from the horizon. Simon had never been on the sea at sunrise. He stopped fishing and started to watch the beauty of the morning. When the stronger beams lightened the mountain, the dark green cover of the hills became apparent. A golden crown changed the nature again. It was reddish-yellow around the boat; the golden road on the water reached them.

When the sun rose completely, it was the end of the dream. Fishing time was over. Simon had not caught anything, but he would never forget the magical change in nature. When they came to shore, Simon thanked Vahram. The brightness he had lived in the darkest days could not be repaid with simple gratitude. He squeezed a Byzantium gold coin into Vahram's palm.

"Let the Lord make you richer. You are too generous to a poor fisherman."

Do you think you are poor, my friend? Do you consider me rich?
I wish I was a fisherman instead of governor.
To live in a simple hut, leaving all the grandeur,
I would like to go fishing instead fighting on the land.
Each beauty of nature I would love as my friend.
Scent of the seaweeds on shore friendly for a good breath,
Phosphorescence on the sea, friendly to find the path,
Screams of the seabirds pushing the magic away
Are sure friendly for early warning, a new day.
My poor fisherman friend, don't complain. You are happier than us
and surely the richest.

Simon went to the port to meet the ship owner with whom he had bargained. "Good morning, Captain Leonardo. Is there any news about our ship?"

"Not yet, Governor Simon. It is late, but don't worry. Your places are reserved."

"When should I come for information?"

"Don't bother at all. I know where you live. I will come and inform you."

Simon was disappointed, but there was nothing he could do.

While Surpik was preparing the lunch table, they heard a noise from the gate.

Vahram said, "A man called Leonardo wants to see you, Governor Simon."

Leonardo collapsed in a chair. "I am ruined, Governor Simon. They sank my ship and its load."

"Who sank it? How did you get this information?"

"My ship was cruising with another vessel. They were attacked on the way. The other one was faster and escaped. My ship was slower and sank in front of the crew." Leonardo was crying.

Simon asked, "Did anyone see who the offender was?"

"My friend told me that it was the Mamluk Navy. He thinks Baybars is on his way to Antioch. His navy must be on duty to block any help."

"Captain Leonardo, tell me who your friend is and where I can find him."

"Everybody knows Captain Franco. He must be in the port now."

Simon said, "Come on, Angelique. We are going to the port."

They ran to the port. Unloading a ship could take days. It was important to find the proper man.

The port master was an old friend of the Legrand family.

Angelique said, "Uncle Marcel, we are looking for a man called Franco. Where can we find him?"

The port master stood up and pointed to a ship disappearing on the horizon. "Franco left the port two hours ago. That ship belongs to him."

Simon asked, "How could he leave the port before unloading?"

"Franco was scared. He decided to quit the business to save his life."

"Would an unloaded ship not lose her speed and create additional risk?"

"He keeps on going by throwing his cargo to the sea. He wanted to save time."

Simon said, "Can we find another ship in this port?"

"No way, Governor Simon. You won't find any ship or any captain here. I shall leave for Cilicia tomorrow. Either I die on the way—or I save my life."

Angelique said, "Thank you, Uncle Marcel. I wish you safe journey."

"Don't mention it, my love. Let me see you once more. We may not see each other again."

At home, dinner was ready. The servants had not left. Nobody was talking or had any appetite.

Angelique recalled old happier days when dinners had lasted two hours. They finished in half an hour and went their room. She threw herself into bed and started to cry.

Simon held her hands and said, "Don't cry, Angelique. We might still have a chance. We are very close to the end. Baybars fell on us like a dark cloud in a storm."

"Don't lose your courage, my love. There are ways out of trouble."

"What can brave sheep do against hungry wolves, Simon? In the first Crusade, the Turks in Antioch were brave. They stood nine months against us, but none of them escaped."

"They lost because there was a traitor among them. We won't have such a man."

Angelique put her arms around Simon and whispered, "There will always be a traitor—everywhere and every time. There will always be winners and losers. I feel we shall be among the losers this time." She put her head on Simon's shoulder. She was crying. "How I have loved you, Simon. I have dreamed of happy lives with you. We lost it all."

Simon did not let Angelique talk more. Their lips joined. He kissed her cheek, ears, and neck. The magic of love made them forget their troubles.

Simon looked into her eyes. There was no fear—only passion. "Angelique, my love, if we have really lost our future, nobody can take today away from us. If there are traitors among us, we have nourished the most beautiful love in our hearts. Let us forget all threats before us. Let us live today with all its beauties."

Angelique kissed him again.

They woke up early, but there was no ship to sail them to happiness. They had no chance but to go back and share the sorrows of their beloved ones. They bade farewell to Vahram's family. They would return to Antioch and its misery.

"Angelique, how do you feel, my love? We can go back to our country."

"I am scared, my darling, but it is not as sorry as it could be. I have lived the greatest happiness with you. I listened to the voice of my heart and explored the beauties of my body. If I die soon, I will not regret my life—even for a short period of time. What are your thoughts, Simon?"

"Soldiers are those who sacrifice their lives for love. We register for the army out of love of our country. We stand against difficulties for love of duty. We become heroes to honor our beloved ancestors. We fight to save our loving friends and for the comfort of our lovely families behind us. If you ask me, after I met you, I understood how there were loves above military and patriotic considerations. Those loves are worth a long life. I have seen a lot of dying soldiers. They were happy and proud. If that happens to me, I will be proud of loving you." He kissed her.

In the last week of April, Prince Bohemond was in a meeting with his officers and governor. "As you all know, Baybars moved to Tripoli. If he is defeated there, we shall avoid a huge disaster. They asked for our help. I will send half our forces to there to help. When I will am away, Simon will replace me as usual."

After the Bohemond forces entered Tripoli, Baybars came on. When he learned from his spies that half of the Antioch forces were in the castle, he changed his mind and turned to Antioch, which was caught unprotected.

The first week of May, Simon woke up in the palace. They had moved there because of the absence of Bohemond.

"Simon, I want to tell something that will please you. I am pregnant."

Simon did not know how to react. The happiest news of his life had come at a difficult time. "Are you sure, Angelique? I cannot define how happy I am. I hope our baby will bring us luck."

They went to breakfast cheerfully. Their mood was spoiled by screams from the gate.

"Governor, I have bad news. The army occupied Seleucia Pieria and is moving toward Antioch."

Angelique's face paled, and her hands started to tremble. Nobody could console her. "The memories of my childhood, youth, and happiest moments of my love have all gone. What happened to our servants, Vahram, my room, and my garden?

In May 1268, Mamluk's army appeared in front of Antioch. People watched the siege from the mountain. Angelique ran to the church to see her parents. Many citizens gathered in the garden to pray.

Simon entered into the garden and climbed up to a high floor to deliver his speech. "Citizens, Antioch is under siege. Unfortunately, the prince is away. Under the circumstances, we shall try to protect you and our city with all our forces. We hope Bohemond will be back during this time—or we get support from a friendly neighbor. If the worst comes true—and no help comes in time—we shall all be in danger. My advice is to hide in the caves with some food and precious belongings. If they enter the city, it will be most harmful during the first days. God bless you."

When Simon got down, he walked directly to the Legrand family.

"Mrs. Legrand, Mr. Legrand. It was an honor to meet you. Marrying Angelique was the greatest happiness of my life. Unfortunately, it may be time to fall apart."

Roland said, "We have been honored to meet you as well. Antioch did not bring you luck. You may wish you had not come here at all."

"You are wrong, Mr. Roland. If I was born ten more times and knew that each time I would confront with Mamluks, I would still like to be here if Angelique was here. Who can escape from death? Everybody dies sooner or later. Maybe soldiers die little bit earlier, but a woman like Angelique is so hard to find that it's worth dying ten times."

Angelique embraced Simon and burst into tears.

Simon took her to a quiet corner and said, "Angelique, from now on, you should stay with your parents. Tomorrow I shall try a surprise attack on the Mamluks. If I succeed, we may be out of this disaster. If I fail, we may not be together again. Don't forget my soul will always be with you. Feel me near you. If you are alone, talk to me. No matter how much trouble you face, stand for me. Survive any torture for our baby. Maybe I will not take my baby in my arms, but I will be sure that you will always try to provide a good life for the dearest fruit of our love. Our baby will be born to make humans happy. Angelique, please keep our baby alive." He kissed his wife and ran away before he saw the tears in her eyes.

In the morning, Antioch's army gathered behind the walls. Simon had planned a surprise attack when the enemy was asleep. He wanted to kill Baybars and some of his commanders. They attacked the opening of the gate, and there were no soldiers to stop them. They were progressing easily. Had Mamluks been entrapped?

They looked up and saw hundreds of archers encircling them. Soldiers were falling under the rain of arrows. Simon ordered an immediate retreat, but it was too late. On the way back, there were plenty of Mamluk soldiers. Simon recalled Angelique's words. A traitor had emerged and sold them. Simon ordered them to put down their arms. After the failure, nobody heard about him.

Angelique and her family were in their garden. They were getting ready to hide in the mountain. They took their valuables and enough food and water to keep them alive for few days. They bade farewell to the church servants and started to climb Silpius Mountain.

Angelique had known many of the caves since she was a child. While climbing, they met many citizens trying to hide. Near the peak, Angelique found a large cave for herself and her mother. She found another cave for her father with a tunnel. They could store their food in his cave, and there were a lot of herbs in the meadow. It was cold at night, but they had blankets. Angelique pulled her blanket around her. She did not feel the cold, but she was embarrassed by her thoughts. They had left the house and church where their family had lived for 170 years. Their summer resort did not exist anymore. The fate of the man who had given her the greatest happiness was unknown.

The next day, they watched the army enter the city. In a very short time, thousands poured in the city. They rushed into the houses to loot whatever valuables they could find. They killed the men right away and dragged the women and children to the square to be sold as slaves. The houses were being set on fire. Flames were ascending to the sky. Angelique watched the extinction of her beautiful city. Soldiers came to the church and her house. Angelique watched her memories burn and a brilliant history turn into ash. The palace was saved for last. Angelique recalled Simon's words: *When Baybars comes here, heaven will turn into hell.*

Angelique and Helen left their cave at night. Because their food was in Roland's cave, they were hungry all day. They had dinner together and thought about the future.

Roland said, "We'll stay hidden tomorrow for our safety, but we cannot wait longer. Our food will run short and Mamluks will search the mountain. After resting the whole day, we should try to reach the other side through the tunnel. I hope no soldier stays that long."

Helen said, "You suggest a clever thing, Roland, but then what?"

"If we can reach Amanos Mountain in the darkness, we will be safe."

The family implemented the plan. The shock of the previous night was over. They slept well.

In the morning, there was silence all around. The soldiers must have been tired. When the sun rose, they hid the entry of their caves with brush.

It was a quiet day. The sky was darkening after sunset. There were only a small number of soldiers inside the walls. The rest were in the headquarters. They had gathered enslaved women and children outside the walls. They were sitting or lying on the ground. Roland estimated the number to be one hundred thousand. The Mamluks had not killed them. They were for sale.

As darkness grew, they were more excited. They finished all the food before moving. They came to the rescue tunnel, which went straight to the other side with some large chambers in between. Between the last chamber and the exit, there was a narrow slope. It was slightly difficult but worth trying.

Roland, Helen, and Angelique crawled through the passage. They came to the last chamber without any problems. It was large enough to hold three people. Roland took the lead for the difficult part. Helen pushed him to ease his climb. Angelique was doing the same to help her mother. Roland touched the ground and pulled himself out into the fresh air. He was as happy as the victorious commanders. Helen held the edges of the hole. Before pulling herself up, she waited for her husband's call. She had not seen the soldiers behind the hole. Unfortunately, it was too late for Roland. When he stood up, a spear hit his back.

"I am trapped, Helen. Turn back. I was shot."

A soldier noticed someone in the passage. "Yusuf, I think there is somebody else."

The soldier who shot Roland was emptying his pockets, but the other two ran to the hole.

Helen yelled, "Angelique, go back quickly."

Helen pushed her daughter with her feet. Angelique fell back into the chamber. If Helen tried to escape, they would find Angelique. She could not bear to see Angelique in trouble. She had to gain time to save Angelique. She waited at the hole. A soldier stretched his hand and grabbed Helen's hair.

The scream alerted the other soldier. He helped pull Helen up by her arms. Finding a beautiful woman in the passage pleased them so much that they did not think to look for another one. They pushed Helen on the ground and tore off her dress. While one was raping Helen, the other one was biting her legs and breasts.

While her cries were getting louder, Angelique realized how brave her mother was. She cried until she was exhausted. Her heart and her body were in pain. She could not move her legs, hands, or neck. A hard cramp had almost paralyzed her. She was only able to think. A week earlier, she'd had a loving husband, caring parents, and a relaxing home. She thought nothing was worth living for. She wanted to share her mother's destiny. She started to climb up to the hole—until she heard Simon's voice: *No matter how much trouble you face, stand for me. Survive any torture for our baby.*

Was it real or dream? Angelique felt that she was not alone. She had the divine responsibility of being a mother. She recalled her mother's sacrifice. She had to survive through all tortures for her baby. "Simon, darling, our baby will be born. I shall give a life and provide a future for our baby. Our baby will possess something we never had."

She came back from the tunnel. She came back to life. She heard voices in the cave. She saw Mamluk soldiers approaching. She saw hidden people move out in panic, but nothing happened to them. She thought she could be safer moving in the daytime.

A soldier told her to walk down to the plain. Angelique regretted being hidden and tried to escape. Her parents had lost their lives in vain. The soldiers split them into two groups: young women and others. They were led to a huge plain outside the city walls.

The soldiers were treating Angelique's group nicely. They were supplying food and water regularly. The only discomfort was the obligation to sleep on the ground, which was not a problem on hot summer nights. All the girls in her group recognized the wife of the governor and did their best to make life easier for her.

A day later, some people on horses and coaches came to the gathering place. They were watching the slaves and buying them with

Byzantine gold. By sunset, half the slaves were sold. After dinner, they were informed they would leave Antioch the next day. Nobody knew what would happen to them. They planned to ship the beautiful young girls to Alexandria to sell them at the best prices.

The next day, the group walked thirty kilometers with no food and arrived at the port late that evening. The ships were ready. They were given food, water, and resting time before leaving.

Angelique rested in the shade with four new friends. She was dreaming of her house and her happiest moments. After dinner was served by the soldiers, Angelique went to put on her shoes. She took two steps and staggered with an unbearable pain in her right foot. The girl next to her saw the poisonous snake and crushed its head with a big stone. When a soldier pressed the swelling on her leg, Angelique screamed.

"She was bitten by a poisonous snake. The girl will die in two hours. Take the others onto the vessel. Leave her here so she does not create a problem on the boat."

After the last group left, Angelique was alone on the shore. The bruise turned to purple, and her pain was growing by the moment. She tore a piece of cloth from her dress and wrapped the bruise. Her pain was bearable, but she was thirsty. She recalled a stream forty meters away. The road to the stream was a rocky slope. It was difficult to reach with her aching foot.

No matter how much trouble you face, stand for me. Survive any torture for our baby.

She started to crawl toward the stream. A big stone stopped her. It was impossible to pass this hurdle. A strong spasm increased her pain. After breathing deeply, she stepped on her left foot. She stuck her fingers into the holes of the rock and pulled herself up. She fainted on the rock. After some rest, she started to creep again. She cried from a pain in her palm. In the darkness, she had touched a stinging nettle. Her palm was burning, but she was going to reach the water. She did not have much hope, but she had incredible drive.

When she finally reached the stream, she drank till she was satisfied.

She stuck her leg into the cold water. Her pain was frozen. Her heartbeat slowed down. She had difficulty breathing.

"Simon, darling, forgive me. I could not save our baby."

"Angelique, is it you? Where are you?"

"Here I am, sweetheart. I'm coming to you." She saw a shadow in the darkness and was pleased. "Simon?"

"Angelique, it's me. Vahram. What happened to you?"

Angelique was amazed. "I was bitten by a snake."

Vahram was at work immediately. He pressed his mouth to the bruise and sucked with all his strength. He repeated this action several times. He carried her to an ancient grave of an old king. He made a bed for her and burned a dry branch. He cauterized the bruise. He put some herbs on the swelling and wrapped it. He tried to pour some soup in her mouth.

"I am shivering, Vahram. My teeth are chattering."

"You recognized me, Angelique. Don't worry anymore. You will be all right."

14

Destination Konya

In the mist of the morning, Angelique was sweating. The wool she was wearing had become too heavy. She got rid of it by turning around. She was awakened to reality. She recalled what had happened to her. Vahram was sleeping near her. She stood up to urinate. She put her left knee on the ground. She carefully stepped on her right leg. She felt a slight pain and left the chamber. Breathing clean air helped her move.

She sat on a rock and thought. When she lost her parents and husband, she found her old friend. After the sting of the snake, she had returned to life miraculously. Her old friend with the broken heart had been her savior. She had never lived such a contrast of feelings—pain joy, regret, obligation, threat, and security. Could all these sentiments be felt at the same time?

Vahram said, "Angelique, how are you? Since you walked so far, you seem to be all right."

"Thank you, Vahram. You saved my life. I will never forget this."

"You are my childhood friend. What I did for you is not worth mentioning."

"Okay, but what were you doing in the tunnel?"

"I was fishing the day before the occupation. When I got home, the mansion was on fire. I turned back to a small bay two miles away. I was worried about my parents. If they were alive, they would search for me

119

there. When nobody came, I felt grief. I lost all hope. I decided to stay one more day. When I thought I was lonely, I heard a voice. When I followed it, I found you."

"We are alive at the moment, but how long can we survive? How can we escape? Can we go to your uncle on the boat? We can catch fish."

"What you suggest is impossible, Angelique. The coastline is under the control of the navy. I don't think occupying Antioch will satisfy Baybars. He can move to Cilicia and central Anatolia."

"Will we not be able to escape him wherever we go?"

"Our sole chance is to get away from the routes the Mamluks will follow. They are a big army. They cannot pass over mountains. They have to follow the coastline. We should climb the mountains. They may turn left to sack Cilicia. We should turn right to Marasion. We can safely proceed into Armenian territory. For our real rescue, we should arrive in Central Anatolia—in Caesarion, for instance. Even then, there is a possibility that Baybars can stretch his forces that far. Our only real chance will be Konya."

"Vahram, you almost described the return route of the Crusaders."

"Maybe it is divine destiny. In order for the forgiveness of the sins the Crusaders committed, one of their grandchildren must follow the opposite way."

"Okay, Vahram. When shall we set out?"

"When we pass through the Titus Tunnel, we'll have to walk till Pieria Mountain on a flat plain. That is the most difficult stage of our escape. We'll risk being noticed. It is still dark. Can you start walking now or do you need to rest?"

"It is not the time to wait, Vahram. I am all right. Let's go."

Vahram put his belongings into his saddlebag.

Angelique was so scared she forgot her pain. She walked quickly—sometimes even in front of Vahram. They soon passed the tunnel, and there was a meadow before the forest. If the soldiers had been around, they would see them easily. Luckily, nobody was patrolling. They tried to follow the paths close to the bushes. When they finally reached the forest, they rested.

Vahram broke a thick branch to protect them against the wild animals. "We came to rest. The threat is mostly over, but if you are not tired, I say we better walk another hour. We shall be safer this way."

"I can walk, Vahram. Farther is safer for us."

In the forest, there were a lot of strange sounds. Angelique was afraid of wild animals, but she kept walking. The army was more frightening then any wilderness. When she was exhausted, she supported herself against a tree.

Vahram found some blackberries. They ate fruit for lunch and kept on walking. When it got dark, they slept beneath some pine trees. Vahram prepared beds on large branches. It was not easy to sleep, but Angelique had no complaints. For the first time in days, she felt safe.

"Get up, Angelique. It's breakfast time."

"What do we have to eat?"

"I picked some wild pears and found some honey. Our water is clean from the stream."

Angelique got down from the tree and washed her face in the stream. The pears were not ripe but were good with the honey.

Vahram filled their bottles with clean water. "We shall walk to Belen Mountain today. We should not be close to any villages till Marasion. We do not know if the people here are friendly or hostile."

They arrived in Marasion in four days without any problems and were welcomed warmly by Vahram's childhood friend and his mother.

The old woman said, "Did you get any news from your father and mother, Vahram?"

"No, Aunty Siranush. Most probably they were murdered. Baybars kills everybody except those who can be sold in slave markets. Angelique's mother and father were killed the same way. Did you get any news from Cilicia, Leon?"

"Yes. Mamluk's army proceeded to Kozan, sacking all the cities on the way and killing everybody. You made a good decision to come here."

"How long will this place be safe, Leon?" asked Angelique.

"Nobody can know for sure. I think at least a year. He took Antioch. He sacked Cilicia. His army must be tired and is far away."

"Why should he return, Leon? Is it easy to come back here? He may spend the winter in Antioch or Cilicia."

Leon asked, "What do you plan to do?"

"I believe we can be safe if get to Konya or Caesarion. What do you say?"

"You are right, Vahram, but from here to Caesarion takes at least ten days."

"If you knew how afraid we were, you would see it's worth trying."

They stayed for three days. Leon provided them with everything they would need for the journey. They filled their saddlebags. They proceeded north for three days and turned left. They spent nights in *caravanserais*. Vahram had spent the Byzantium gold he had taken from Simon. Close to the Caesarion they saw a very big *caravanserai*.

It was dark, and they were tired. They entered through a gate into a big backyard with rooms all around.

An old man approached and said, "Welcome, youngsters. Where did you come from? Where are you going?"

Vahram said, "We came from Antioch. We ran away from Baybars."

"I think you want to stay. Are you married?"

Vahram looked at Angelique for a moment and said, "We are married. We want to stay, but we do not know if we can afford the price."

The innkeeper looked at them with pity. "This is Karatay Caravanserai. By the order of Seljuk Sultan Giyaseddin Keyhusrev, passengers can stay here for three days free of charge. We mend their shoes, take care of their horses, and treat their wounds. If you are not passengers with a known address, you can stay and work here. We need employees."

Angelique said, "You are right, innkeeper. We are running away from Baybars. He killed our parents, and we have no place to go. If you give us jobs, we will work with all our loyalty."

"You are tired and hungry tonight. You should eat and sleep now. I'll see you tomorrow."

The next day, they were awakened by the servants. Hasan Dayi waited for them at the breakfast table.

After a good meal, Hasan Dayi said, "Angelique, you will clean the rooms with Nezahat. When you finish, you will help with laundry. You pick up the dishes on the tables after lunch and dry the washed dishes. You do the same after dinner, and your job is finished. Vahram, you will wash and clean the corridors and yard. You will carry incoming and outgoing goods. You will help the horse keepers and boiler attendants in / charge of baths. You will serve our guests and distribute their drinks."

Angelique would start earlier and finish earlier than Vahram. They were given clean work dresses. When they went back in their room, they were tired but happy.

At night, they pushed apart the beds to hide their unmarried status. Their third day at the inn was bathing day for the servants. Vahram and Angelique washed in separate rooms. They washed away the dirt and were relaxed. Angelique's pink cheeks were unbearable for Vahram. They pushed her bed to the other corner of the room. She got in bed, but he sat near her.

"You are so beautiful, Angelique, that I can't keep myself from looking at you."

Angelique did not know what to do.

"Angelique, I have loved you always. When Simon was in our way, I could not confess this. I kept myself away from you, but our routes always intersect. We lost everything and stayed alone. Our survival depends on our togetherness. Can't you love me after all we have lived?"

Angelique said, "Vahram, I always loved you as my brother. I cannot forget what you did to me. Had you not been by my side I would not be here today. You saved me from all dangers, but I am not ready to love as you mean. Please be sensitive and give me some time."

Vahram collapsed. His passion for Angelique had made him crazy. "I have waited for this moment for years. I believed our destiny would tie us one day. We are on that day now. Why are you waiting? We have nobody else on earth."

"If you really love me, we should not have any relationship beyond the holy marriage ties. There are some priests coming to the inn. I will ask them to marry us secretly."

Vahram said, "Oh my darling, I cannot explain how happy I am. All my troubles have ended. I am like a traveler in the desert finding water after days of thirst. I am like the sinner ascended from hell to heaven with the mercy of the Lord."

Vahram went to his bed and slept happily.

The next day, there was an unfamiliar activity at the inn. Three Mongolians came from Caucasus as representatives of Abaka Khan. Many principalities and Seljuk sultans were now under Mongolian protection of Abaka Khan in Anatolia. The men were treated exclusively everywhere. When Angelique went to their room for cleaning, the head of the group was there.

The tall man with a dirty moustache watched Angelique. Angelique was disturbed by his stares. She finished her work quickly and left. When she told her story to Vahram that night, he was not in a mood to pay attention. He had convinced one of the priests at the inn to marry them.

Angelique called Nezahat before going to the leader's room and requested that she accompany her for the cleaning. When the two women entered the room, two soldiers attacked on them.

Nezahat screamed and collapsed when one of them fell on her. Her mouth was bleeding. The soldier covered Nezahat. The other two pushed Angelique onto the bed. While one of tore off her dress, the other held her arms and tried to stop her shouting. When Angelique was completely naked, one soldier rode on her. Angelique was hardly breathing.

The door opened, and Vahram appeared with a hay fork in his hand. He stabbed the Mongol on her back with his tool. The other soldier wanted to interfere, but he was too late. Vahram grabbed the sword near the bed and pierced the second soldier's abdomen. He pushed the man on Angelique to the floor. While he tried to take care of Angelique, the one on Nezahat lifted his sword.

Vahram noticed the soldier and tried to protect himself, but what could a poor peasant do against a trained soldier. He lost his sword with one swing, and the soldier approached.

Nezahat realized the tragedy. She took a spear from the wall and approached from behind. The Mongolian soldier sliced Vahram's abdomen before Nezahat stabbed the soldier with the spear.

The door opened, and Hasan Dayi entered with two of his men. They were amazed by the scene. Hasan Dayi pulled himself together quickly. He closed the door and covered Angelique's naked body; she was waking up from her shock. He saw Nezahat and the dead bodies of the soldiers.

When Angelique noticed Vahram with the sword stuck in his belly, she ran to him. "Darling, what happened to you? Vahram, please don't die. Don't leave me alone."

"I feel cold, Angelique. Please hold me and warm me up."

"I am, darling. I will not leave you to die."

"I am happy you are safe."

Angelique put the dead body on the bed and started to cry.

Nezahat told the whole story to Hasan Dayi.

The innkeeper said, "Omar, rush to the bakery. Pick up four big sacks of flour and bring them here. The chief security guard, Konya Rukneddin, is there. Find him and fetch him. Enough, Angelique. Don't cry. You cannot bring a dead man back to life."

Angelique looked up toward Hasan Dayi. The corpse was gone. There was a tall man with Hasan Dayi. Two men held her arms and dragged her to Hasan Dayi's room.

"Angelique, I want to introduce you to Rukneddin, the chief security guard of Konya. I told him what happened to you. We both think it is not possible for you to stay here. We got rid of the Mongol corpses, but they may have friends who will investigate the case."

"Hasan Dayi, I have nobody in my life. Where can I go?"

"Angelique, we are never alone. The Lord is always with us. Whenever you feel lonely, talk to him. Whatever you have a problem, consult him. Rukneddin will depart for Konya tomorrow. He can take you with him."

"But where can I found somebody else whose heart is full of love?"

"If the Lord plans it for you, Angelique, you can find someone much greater than me. You can meet the sultan of hearts. You can reach the source of love. Don't worry. I shall pray for you."

They set out early in the morning. Angelique was happy to find a home with the loving people there, but she was on another journey to the unknown.

On the third evening, they arrived at Rukneddin's house. His wife was embarrassed when she learned that Angelique would stay permanently, but she could not object to her husband.

15

Words of Tolerance

Rukneddin's house was a two-level house in the middle of a garden. In the large dining room, there were two doors—one to kitchen, the other to the bath and toilet. On the second floor, there were four large bedrooms.

The chief guard had a nineteen-year-old son at home. His two daughters were married and away. Three servants were in the garden. Angelique was given a couch in the annex. Her duties were feeding and milking two cows, getting water from the well, washing the laundry, watering the flowers, and cleaning the house.

That evening, Angelique was in the fold talking to the cows. "My beautiful girl, move out to the side so I can clean the floor. Good yellow girl, don't be as naughty as your sister. Okay, good. You both deserve plenty of hay tonight."

Angelique did not notice the guard's son.

Burhaneddin said, "I heard you talking to the cows, Angelique. Do they understand you?"

"Maybe not, but they do whatever I say."

"I really saw it, but how could it happen?"

"Animals do not know our language, but they know a caring person from the voice."

"Are there other creatures who listen to your loving words?"

"The power of love is effective for all creatures. You can influence plants, for instance."

"Can you show me how you do it, Angelique?"

She put all the dung she collected in a bucket and brought it to the rose garden.

Burhaneddin followed her.

She hoed the soil at the bottom of the roses and cut off the dried branches. She poured the dung below and started watering. She said, "Good morning, beautiful plant. What nice buds you have. I want you to have colorful flowers next time. I will give you plenty of water so you will not fade away and dry."

Burhaneddin watched her in amazement. He had first been caught by her beauty, but he gradually understood that she had something more than physical beauty.

Angelique talked to the cows while she milked them. They stayed quiet while she filled two buckets.

Burhaneddin helped her carry the buckets to his mother in the kitchen.

Hurrem could not believe there were two full buckets of milk. "Did you add yesterday's milk to today's?"

"No, Mom. Angelique milked them all today. I saw it with my own eyes."

Rukneddin noticed the roses in the garden and said, "I have never seen these roses bloom so beautifully. Hurrem, what happened this year?"

"Angelique does it. She talks to them. She also gets more milk from the cows by talking to them. I saw it with my own eyes."

"Do you follow Angelique all day long?"

"No, Mom. I saw it accidentally."

"You came to the kitchen last week with her. Was that accidental too?"

Burhaneddin's father said, "If our son helped a young girl carry a heavy load, what's wrong with this? Angelique is a poor girl who escaped from the cruelty of Baybars. She has been entrusted to me by Hasan Dayi."

"If it is so, should you keep her in your house? Why don't you give her to one of your friends and let her stay there. Do you want an infidel to be our daughter-in-law?"

Hurrem's grandfather was a longtime servant in the Seljuk's palace. Rukneddin was cautious with his wife. If his son married a Christian, it would not be well received.

"Okay, I will try to find somebody for her."

The answer pleased Hurrem, but it upset Burhaneddin.

"Be quick. It will be more difficult to depart later."

When Rukneddin was alone, he started to think. He had to send her to a reliable place. In Meram, there were places for dining and entertaining rich people and high-ranking officers. Since they were owned by the viziers, they were reliable. Vizier Ziyaeddin Han was under the management of an experienced lady. He had known her for a long time. Tavus used to play a very good harp for her exclusive customers and organized dinner parties with quality wine, music, and belly dancers. If Rukneddin gave Angelique to Ziyaeddin Han, he would have to visit her since he was responsible for her. Hurrem gladly accepted the idea.

Rukneddin said, "Look Angelique, I am very satisfied with your service and respectful behavior. Unfortunately, I cannot provide a comfortable life for you here. I am deeply sorry that you have to work in the fold with the cows."

"Don't worry at all. Humans can be happier in hay than in palaces."

Rukneddin did not know what to say. He had expected complaints from her and had prepared his speech accordingly. "Still … I wish you lived in more comfortable conditions—if I could find a better place."

"Do you plan to send me to somebody else?"

"Don't misunderstand me, Angelique. I want you to stay with one of my friends where I believe you will be more comfortable."

Angelique was sad, but she said, "As you wish. When are we going?"

This was another unexpected answer. "If you want, we can visit my friend after breakfast."

"Let me pick up my dresses and bid farewell to the cows. I'll come down."

"Do you want to see your friends?"

"No one is my friend. They did not want me here, but the cows will surely miss me."

Burhaneddin said, "I always wanted you to stay with us Angelique."

"I know, but it is time to depart."

"Can I visit you?" Rukneddin said.

"It does not matter to me. Ask your parents."

When Angelique entered the private room of Tavus at the Han, she was dazzled by the magnificence. Even the Seljuk's palace was dull compared to here. When Tavus entered the room, Angelique's worries disappeared.

"Welcome to Ziyaeddin Han, Angelique. I learned from the chief security guard what happened to you at Karatay Caravanserai. I always need people to work. If you work for me, I shall be pleased. You will be comfortable and make money.

Angelique said, "As long as you want to keep me, I work for you. I don't have any other choice. My comfort and making money are not important factors. I lived the most grievous moments when I was at my happiest. I came across evil incidents after my days of luxury. I found happiness when I was hopeless. Why is our comfort important if we are not sure about tomorrow? What good is making money if it will be confiscated by tyranny?"

Tavus said, "You have greatly influenced me, Angelique. I will assign you as my first assistant. I have owned everything in life, but I have no real friends. I smiled many times when I was crying in my heart. As soon as I saw you, I knew you were special. I have waited for years. Your beauty can only be dreamed of by angels. The wisdom in your words can only be heard by saints."

Angelique's job was to make sure that dinner, entertainment, rooms, and service were perfect. The tiring job required sixteen hours on some days, but Angelique did not complain. She loved Tavus like an elder sister. She went to her room every night and chatted for hours.

Tavus enjoyed life for the first time. With Angelique, she did not need to worry about anything. Angelique was considerate and serious. The servants supervised by Angelique admired her. They had never been treated so gently or justly. The customers visited the Han more frequently. Some of them used to come just to watch her beauty.

If she entered the big dining hall and saw Rukneddin and his son, she did not change her manner even slightly.

Hurrem was in her garden with Ibrahim's wife.

Makbule Hatun said, "How wonderful your roses are this year."

Hurrem said, "Rukneddin brought a girl from Karatay. She took care of them."

"Can you send her to us? Our roses are bad this year."

"She is not with us. She is an assistant for Tavus."

"My uncle met your husband and son last week at Ziyaeddin Han. A beautiful girl was serving them. Her name was something like Angel. Is she the one you mention?"

Hurrem was in shock. While she tried to rescue her son, she was losing her husband. She turned her head to hide her anger. "She might be. Since she was entrusted by Hasan Dayi, he checks on her sometimes."

Makbule kept talking, but Hurrem's mind was stuck on Angelique. She was unable to think about anything else. She had to solve this.

––––––––––––

Judge Ibrahim arrived early at his office and greeted Hurrem and two men.

"Good day, Hurrem Hatun. What are you doing here so early?"

"Judge Ibrahim, don't ask me what happened to us. An infidel came to Ziyaeddin Han. She leads the men of Muslim women to prostitution. My husband and son are trapped. Please find a solution to this situation."

"Prostitution is an important crime, Hurrem Hatun. Have you seen it occur?"

"God save me from going to those kind of places, but I have two witnesses."

Judge Ibrahim addressed her companions. "Have you seen this lady engage in prostitution?"

"Yes, Judge Ibrahim. We had fun with her. Her name is Angelique."

"I should know your identities to determine whether you are reliable witnesses."

One man stepped ahead and bowed. He said, "I am Hashim. The chief hostler of the horses in the palace. God forgive me for my sins with Angelique."

"I am Mustafa, my judge, the wine keeper of the sultan. I did the same as Hashim."

Judge Ibrahim turned to the scribe and said, "Write, Ali. It has been confirmed by the testimonies of two reliable witnesses that Ziyaeddin Han's employee, Angelique, committed prostitution. She will be punished by a hundred lashes. Two guards should go to the Han, bring her here, and whip her in the square."

Hurrem shivered with happiness. Those who suffered this punishment seldom survived. If they did, they had to leave Konya. She had rescued her husband and son.

At Ziyaeddin Han, the servants were preparing the tables for lunch. Two security guards entered through the gate. They read the summons to Tavus.

Tavus was shocked. Once more, an innocent girl was a victim of slander. She had to rush to save Angelique. She said, "Relax. I will send you beverages while I will fetch her."

Tavus found Angelique immediately.

"Angelique, my dear, somebody slandered you as a prostitute. The punishment of this crime is one hundred lashes. Most do not survive. I don't know who slandered you, but you must run away quickly."

"I know it is Hurrem, but I don't want to run away. I'd rather die and be free of my troubles."

"No, my love, you must try. You should do it for your baby. Would

Simon like you to do so? You have found somebody to help you each time you tried."

"Okay, Tavus, but where can I go? I have no money. What can I do?"

"Go to Meram Gardens and hide behind the trees. In the darkness, go west. There are many Turkish principalities in that direction that are known for their hospitality. In this purse, there are thirty pieces of gold. Take this pelerine on your shoulders to hide your hair. I will try to keep the guards busy. Start running."

"Tavus, how can I pay for what you have done for me? I shall try to run away for my baby."

"Okay, darling. Good luck to you."

On hot spring days, people used to picnic along the river in Meram Gardens. Angelique ran there as fast as she could, but one of the guards saw her.

"Huseyin, I am afraid the one we came for is running away. Let's chase after her."

They shouted at her to stop, but Angelique dropped her pelerine and ran faster.

The guards started to close the gap near the river. When they were about to catch her, Angelique saw young men listening to an old teacher. She ran up to the old man and said, "They slandered me. They will whip me. Please help."

The old man lifted her up and covered her with his pelerine.

The two guards stopped in front of the old man. "Mevlana[3], I apologize if we disturbed you. We are after a criminal. We want to take her to Ibrahim."

---

3   Mevlana was born in Belh as the second son of Bahaeddin Veled who used to be called as the sultan of the scholars. The ruler of Horasan was jealous of his fame. A nearing Mongol threat forced him to leave for Nishabur. Mevlana met the great scholar Feriduddin Attar there. Then they went to Bagdat and Mecca where they met illiterate people who believed what they had been told without thinking. Mevlana compared revelations to wisdom and logic. From Mecca, they proceeded to Damascus and Larende in Anatolia. Mevlana married Gevher Hatun, the daughter of a rich man. He stayed in Larende for seven years with his father. He learned Arabic, Persian, Hebrew, Greek, and Latin. He settled in Konya at the end.

The old man called one of his disciples and said, "Husameddin, go to Ibrahim after lunch with our friends to learn about the case. You, my boys, have a rest and be our guests at lunch."

Although Angelique was next to them, the guards did not see her.

Nobody could object to Mevlana Celaleddin, and the court papers were invalidated.

Mevlana took Angelique to his mansion.

Kerra Hatun smiled and said, "Welcome our house, Angelique. From now on, it is your home as much as ours."

Angelique adapted to the family in a short time. Her main job was to serve Kerra Hatun, but there were a lot of things to do. There were kitchen, food store, bathroom and many bedrooms for poor residents of the house around the yard for which she would be responsible to clean.

Angelique had found a peaceful life. She was feeding the animals, caring for the flowers, and helping the household, but her happiest times were spent near Kerra Hatun. The woman shared valuable advice. Things were favorable, but the verdict of Judge Ibrahim had not yet been executed.

A few weeks later, there was a meeting at the great reception hall of Regent Sahip Ata Fahreddin Ali. Mevlana, his disciple Husameddin, and Angelique sat on the couches in the hall. Angelique saw a lot of unfamiliar people on the opposite side. At the far end of the room, there was decorated chair for the regent. In the meantime, there were newcomers. Angelique was excited when she saw Rukneddin, Burhaneddin, and Hurrem enter the room. The last visitors before the regent were Vizier Ziyeddin, the owner of the place, and Tavus. They sat near Mevlana.

Regent Sahip Ata came in and said, "We gather here to hear the objection of Husameddin Çelebi to the verdict of Judge Ibrahim on prostitution by the Ziyaeddin Han employee Angelique. Come here Husameddin. Tell us the basis of your objection."

Husameddin said, "My great regent, Angelique abides now at Mevlana's house and serves Kerra Hatun. Formerly, she was the assistant to Tavus at the Han. Those who know her are sure of her honesty. Judge Ibrahim made a fundamental mistake in this trial by listening to two witnesses instead of four."

"Judge Ibrahim, if this is true why did you make decision with only two witnesses?"

Judge Ibrahim said, "His regency, the witnesses were reliable persons from the court, and I could not find any others. Considering the public benefit and urgency, I did not want to delay the punishment."

Husameddin said, "If Judge Ibrahim wanted, he could find many witnesses. For instance, I found a lot of witnesses with the opposite opinion."

"Introduce your witnesses, Husameddin."

"My first witness is the owner of the locality—Vizier Ziyaeddin."

The man sitting near Mevlana stood up and bowed before Sahip Ata. "His regency, I saw Angelique many times while serving. I talked to Tavus and our regular customers about her. They confirmed her honesty. Who are the slanderers that blamed her?"

Husameddin said, "My second and third witnesses are Rukneddin and Burhaneddin. Rukneddin saved Angelique from the Mongols at Karatay Caravanserai and kept her in his house for a long time before he gave her to Tavus."

"Rukneddin, come over here with your son and tell me what you know about Angelique."

"His regency, in the short time Angelique worked for us, she earned the love and respect of everybody. After I gave her to Tavus, I visited the house and heard no complaints about her."

Sahip Ata said, "What do you say, Burhaneddin? Do you know Angelique?"

"His regency, when she was working for us, roses were blooming earlier—and the cows were yielding more milk. We have not observed her slightest wrongdoing. Who is the dishonorable one who commits that much sin as to slander an innocent?"

Sahip Ata said, "Ibrahim, tell me who your witnesses were."

"Hashim and Mustafa from the palace are here."

When Sahip Ata called the men, they were pale.

"You were told to make fun of Angelique at Ziyaeddin Han. Is that true?

The servants said, "We might have confused Angelique with someone else at Han."

"So you claim to be at Ziyaeddin Han. Tavus Hatun, come over here and tell us if you know them."

Tavus looked at them. "His regency, I know all our customers. Even if a new one comes, he is brought to me before going to the yard. I have not seen them or heard their names."

Sahip Ata said, "I have heard the case. I make my judgment about the innocence of Angelique. She is found not guilty. Judge Ibrahim's license will be canceled because of his mistake in such an important trial Hashim and Mustafa will be whipped with eighty blows unless they inform their promoter—if there is one."

"We have been promoted by Hurrem Hatun. She offered us money."

Everybody turned to Hurrem.

Rukneddin was furious.

Burhaneddin was amazed.

Sahip Ata said, "Stand up, Hurrem Hatun. Are these accusations correct?"

"Yes, they are. I committed a sin because of jealousy. I wanted to save my husband and son from her, and I slandered her."

"My judgment is corrected. False witnesses Mustafa and Hashim will be whipped forty blows, and Hurrem will be punished with eighty lashes." He stood up to leave.

Angelique said, "Stop please! Since I am the victim, may I request mercy for all?"

Sahip Ata said, "Why do you want mercy for those who acted maliciously against you?"

"His regency, they wanted to be malicious, but they did the greatest favor for me."

Sahip Ata was concerned.

Angelique said, "Had Hurrem not been malicious to me, I would not have been rewarded this way. If Rukneddin had not kicked me out of his home, I would not have found the source of love."

Sahip Ata shivered. He had never heard such tolerant words. He tried to hide his tears. "I forgive all criminals at the request of the victim. God bless Angelique."

Everybody was crying after Sahip Ata left.

Rukneddin shouted, "Angelique was tolerant enough to forgive, but I will not forgive the snake in my bed."

16

Love and Religion

Angelique's trial was the talk of Konya. In the palace and in mansions, everybody was speaking about it. People were chasing any opportunity to meet Angelique.

Mevlana Celaleddin Rumi used to converse with women and men from the upper class on certain days. In one of these meetings, Angelique was among the servants. While the males served the men in the guest chamber, the female servants prepared the meals in the kitchen.

After the visitors arrived, Mevlana entered the room. All the guests lined up to kiss Rumi's hands. Musicians came into the room with flutes, tars, and tambourines.

When the music started, Mevlana permitted his dervishes to whirl.

When Angelique heard the music, she went to see what was happening. She was enchanted.

The next day, Angelique said, "Kerra Ana, some people were dancing yesterday. I was so curious. What was that?"

"That's called *Semag*. It's a kind of worship."

"Is the Moslem ritual worship is not called *namaz*?"

"It is an obligation for all Muslims, but there are times when people feel closer to God. These precious moments change for each of us. If you recollect your creator in those instances, you can get closer to the Lord."

"Are these times shown to us by imams and priests?"

"If you ask them, they can only tell you their own precious moments. If you don't have an abscess on your nape, raise your head to the sky and try to find your creator by yourself. If you search around and listen to the sound of nature, you will see and hear the divine existence everywhere with a special appeal to you."

"Can *Semag* make us hear this voice?"

"It can because rhythm and music are the special languages of God. Humans and animals listen to the same music, but they feel and act differently."

"Okay, Kerra Ana, how did *Semag* come out?"

"Many years ago, Rumi and his disciples were coming back from Medrese, the religious school. They passed through the jewelers' bazaar. In front of a goldsmith's shop, they heard the rhythmic sound of beating gold sheets. The sound enchanted Rumi as if it was the voice of the Lord. With divine instinct, he tried to reach the ultimate lover by whirling. The goldsmith watching Rumi was so inspired that he ordered his apprentices to continue hammering and joined Rumi. After a few turns with Mevlana, he was captured by a transcendental mood. He urged all the watchers to go into his shop to take whatever looked precious to them. He moved to the Medrese and stayed with Mevlana till he died a few years ago. His name was Selahaddin."

Angelique was stunned by the story. "What devotion!"

Mevlana's house was very close to the religious school. Angelique used to go to the school from time to time to distribute food and used gowns to the children of poor families. Some of the wealthy followers of Mevlana also donated regularly. Angelique would ask each recipient about their real needs. If she could not provide those items, she tried to find them for the next time.

In one of these service activities, Angelique heard a sound from inside. She went into the school and started to walk toward the beautiful music. In a large hall, a lonely dervish was playing the tar. If she had not seen it, she would not have believed it. Made from a half a coconut, the three-stringed instrument's sound was echoing and filling the room. The dervish continued playing because he had not noticed Angelique sitting in a corner. When he saw her shadow, he left his instrument and came closer. The dervish thought he was in heaven. A warm feeling of admiration overcame him.

Being unaware of his excitement Angelique said, "How affectionately you play! This is the first time I have seen you."

"My name is Suleiman Çelebi. I teach the tar at the school. I have not seen you before. Who are you?"

"I am Angelique, servant of Kerra Ana. I have recently come to Konya."

"Rumi is my master, and Kerra Hatun is my virtual mother too."

"Then I am glad to meet you. Do you always play here? I'd like to listen to your music again."

"In the mornings, I usually lecture. I prefer to practice in the afternoons when the place is empty. If you come again, I will play for you."

"Thank you. See you next Friday. I am late now and have to rush back."

Angelique listened to Çelebi two more times. Each time, the tar sounded more emotional.

On Friday evening, the women would meet Mevlana. Most of the attendants were from the palace. Rumi came for the conference too.

The visitors heard a noise coming from the gate. Some women were arguing with the guards.

"Great Mevlana, some non-Muslim ladies want to see you."

"Why don't you let them in?"

"Great master, we were not permitted to your meetings because we were not Muslim, but we learned that a Christian lady attended last time. Will you permit us to come listen to you?"

Mevlana stood and opened his arms as if to embrace all human beings with no distinction of religion, race, or gender:

Come whatever is your binding,
Be Buddhist or fire-worshipping.
Break your vow of repenting.
Come again with no despairing.

The ladies were happy since they had heard Angelique's name several times. They felt mutual sympathy for each other. They all listened to Rumi's advice. They discussed the topics of conflict and learned Mevlana's point of view.

One of the women said, "Oh great Rumi, although the Koran and the Bible are said to be the divine words, how come one permits to drink wine and the other forbids? Which one is correct?"

"Both are correct, depending on your character and circumstances of time and place. If your submission to God is as deep as an ocean and you are determined and as firm as a teak tree—or you disturb nobody when you drink and don't lose control—what difference does a glass of wine make? But if your belief in God is as shallow as the water in the glass and your resolution is as rotten as mushroom on wet grass—or are aggressive when you drink—you can tarnish your soul with even one glass of wine."

One of the Muslim women said, "Great Mevlana, our *hocas* (clergy) are not of that opinion."

Mevlana looked at the woman and said, "Why don't you ask these kinds of questions to your conscience instead of asking *hocas*? Why don't you listen to the voice of your heart, the only real house of Allah? Why don't you search for the answers in the Koran, which is the main source of Islam belief, and let people cheat you?"

The wife of one of the important viziers asked, "But if we read the Koran and try to understand it, do you think we can come to a different or better conclusion than the scholars can?"

"Of course," said Mevlana. If you direct your heart to your creator, you can surpass the understanding of the prophets. Moses met a shepherd in a meadow. When he went closer, Moses heard the shepherd praying. 'Oh my beloved God, I love you so much that if you want, I am ready to milk all my sheep and offer you as a drink. If it will please you, I shall clip all the wool of my sheep and make a mantle to protect you from the cold weather. If you are hungry, I will slaughter any of my sheep to feed you.' Moses said, 'Hi, idiot man. God is the sole owner and creator of everything. He is above all human needs. Could he be thirsty or hungry enough to drink milk and eat meat? He surrenders the whole universe. Why could he need your mantle to wear to be protected from the cold?'

"The shepherd was shocked and sad. Moses continued to walk. When Moses slept that night, he heard a divine call in his dream. 'Oh Moses, I gave you the assignment to make me known and loved by my supplicants. What you do separates them from me. You act as if religion is more important than love and not needed by those who love me.' Moses immediately went back to the shepherd and said, 'I am very sorry. All you prayed for is correct. I made a grave mistake in criticizing you. Keep on praying the same way.'"

The women were enchanted and lost in contemplation.

Rumi said, "There was a difference between Moses and the shepherd's understanding of God; the Turkoman and other interpretations of Islam are different too. In the first one, the basis of Islam is love and tolerance. In the others, it is fear and punishment. Non-Turkomans believe that non-Muslims are enemies and must be killed in holy wars. In the Turkmen's attitude, all creatures must be loved because of their creator—and human rights must be preserved. The holy war is not against the enemies; it opposes our own selfishness and egos. The Turks always respected women as sisters, wives, daughters, or heads of state."

Angelique watched the women's eyes sparkle.

Mevlana said, "My advice to you ladies is not to search for God in others. Whatever your question is, the answer is in your heart. God is too immense to be grasped by the minds of fanatics, but he abides in the hearts of lovers. You cannot find divine realities in the past because God changes everything every moment. Those who were omniscient five hundred years ago are ignorant today. Likewise, we shall be that way in five hundred years. The important thing is to remake the judgment every time—based on the knowledge and values of the time.

It's beautiful to wake up each morning with the rising sun.
To live a new formation must be the greatest fun.
No anchoring in a place setting sail on every day,
Arrive in new destinations so apart so long away.

How do nice streams flow never become unclean?
Their water is spotless ever pure and ever serene.
Whatever was told in the past was valid far away.
A new day is this moment something fresh we must say.

Mevlana walked through the long corridor of the school and heard the touching sound of the strings. He turned back and thought that whoever played the tar that movingly must be heartbroken. In the dark room, Mevlana did not recognize the tar player or notice Rumi. Mevlana walked silently and saw Suleiman Çelebi in the corner. He stood up quickly and kissed his hands.

Mevlana kissed Çelebi's head and said, "Good evening, my son. What are you doing here? I was passing by and was stopped by your melodies. I was curious. I turned back and saw you alone in the darkness. Are you sorry for something which you cannot confess to anybody?

Suleiman Çelebi said, "Yes, my master. I have heartache. I am hopelessly in love. I divert myself with music. I talk to my tar and don't know what else to do."

"My son, you are the joy of *Semag* and the master of tar players. Who is she who put you in such grievance? I would like to help you if I can."

"I love Kerra Hatun's servant, master. Angelique loves music and is very kind. She often helps the poor and sometimes comes here to listen to my music. I am a poor dervish and embarrassed to tell her my feelings. I am afraid of losing her."

Rumi did not expect that Çelebi's problem would be so hopeless. His virtual daughter, Angelique, had endured a lot of suffering and disappointment. She was not ready for another love, but he had promised to help Çelebi. He decided to try once. What were Suleiman's real feelings for Angelique? Was he serious about her? Would he be ready to accept her as she is? He wanted to put Çelebi through a hard test.

Oh, my dear Suleiman, do you know what love means?
Will you burn yourself like the firefly?

Can you be as generous as an ocean to your lover?
Will you stay like the dead when you are angry?
Can you act like the dark night and hide your lover's mistakes?
Can you be sunny and show your passionate love?
Are you as modest and kind as the ground you step on?
You look gentle and nice, but is this real?

"Oh, my holy master, if she is your virtual daughter and her baby is your grandchild, how can I refuse them? She stayed alone in life and found you with a divine guidance. How can I not accept her? I am a poor dervish; I am destined to support an unprotected lady. Could there be anything more meritorious than this? Can a dervish be careless with an orphan and act differently to an unborn baby? Can I stand against your teachings about being a good dervish?"

"You have passed the test, Çelebi. Pray that I can convince Angelique to marry you."

A servant called Angelique and said, "Kerra Ana wants to talk you. She is waiting in her room."

When Angelique entered the room, Kerra Hatun was sitting on a big couch with Mevlana. Angelique kissed their hands. Kerra Hatun gave her a big pillow and told her to sit in front of them. Angelique sat with crossed legs on the pillow.

Kerra Hatun said, "Angelique, my dear, although you came here a short time ago, you have gained the respect and love of everybody in this house. You have been very close to Rumi and me. Like all parents, we want to see you happy."

"I am very happy here with you, Kerra Ana."

"We are very happy with you too. We love you as our own daughter. We want to live longer and continue this happiness, but human beings are not immortal. We grow old. We do not want you to be alone or unprotected with your baby. We want you to get married so we will not regret anything."

"Kerra Ana, after experiencing so many mishaps, I am aware of the difficulty of raising a child alone, but I only loved once in my life.

My first love was Simon—and I wanted him to be my last one too. I rejected the love of my closest friend. When my heart is wounded by the loss of my dearest ones and closed to love, how can I lie with a man I will never love?"

Kerra Hatun said, "Your heart is not closed to love, my dear."

You smell the flowers,
Pet animals gently,
Listen to music in a trance,
And say your heart is closed to love?
You show compassion to the elderly.
You run to help the poor.
You care for children on the streets.
And say your heart is closed to love?

Angelique said, "They are different, Kerra Ana. Who would want if I am carrying someone else's child?"

Those who trusted you are never mistaken.
No one has heard you ever tell a lie.
You are never in angry mood.
A man in love will be the one proposing.
He who loves you should know that you're pregnant.
He must see the merit in your deep heart.
He should be gentle, kind, and a master of art.
The tar player will be the one proposing.

Angelique was surprised. Almost every day she went to the school to listen to Suleiman Çelebi's tar, but she had never known his true feelings.

"But I am a Christian. I was born in a church. Whenever I am in trouble, I bow to the Virgin Mary statue and pray."

Mevlana said, "What difference do you see between Muslims and Christians, my girl? What distinguishes your love for Simon from your fascination with the sound of the tar? What is so different between the Virgin Mary's statue and the Koran?"

Angelique did not understand the meaning of Mevlana words.

Rumi said, "Go to the mirror and look at yourself, Angelique."

She stood up and did what she was told.

"Angelique, look into the mirror. Since you love so much, assume that the image you see belongs to Simon. Now turn your back as much as you can and look again. You see a different image, do you not? Since you are careless, assume that what you see is Suleiman."

Angelique was doing whatever Rumi said.

"Turn right and look in the mirror. What you see is Muhammad. Now turn left and look again. This time, you are looking at Christ." Angelique tried to grasp his meaning. "Come here and sit across from me."

Angelique sat cross-legged on the pillow.

Mevlana looked her with love and authority. He lifted his head as if talking to God:

> *Who you think of as Simon or Suleiman is from God.*
> *What you know from Jesus or Mohammed is from God.*
> *All findings in the Bible or Koran are divine knowledge.*
> *The contents of all the books in libraries are from God.*
> *In the fetish of shaman, in statues of Mary,*
> *What you pray in the church and the mosque is from God.*
> *On the palette of a painter, in the breath of a flutist,*
> *In the beat of tambourines, what you perceive is from God.*

Mevlana stood up slowly. Angelique and Kerra Hatun followed him. Mevlana raised up his arms as if praying and continued:

> *In wealth or poverty, in joy or sorrow,*
> *In the mood of all feelings, where you stand is from God.*
> *Birds fly in the sky; fish swim in the oceans.*
> *When bees make us sweet honey, all they do is from God.*

He turned his right palm up and his left palm down and started to whirl. His wife jumped up and took two tambourines from the wall.

Angelique sat on the pillow, took two sticks, and banged the tambourines. Angelique's body was trembling. She did not know what was happening to her, but it sounded familiar.

Kerra Hatun was beating and Mevlana was whirling while he continued his verses:

Sometimes we become sinners; sometimes we do big favors.
You think you do evil or good, but all your deeds are from God.
You seem different from the right; you stand apart from the left.
You only look at your own self; what you see is from God.

Angelique felt a strong desire to join the whirling.

Don't be misled by the sight; don't ever think of any change.
What you love in Simon or Suleiman is from God.
Let's join to the dervishes; let's feel the eternal love.
Let us become all the same, all existence is from God.

Mevlana looked at Angelique and solemnly bowed his head.

Angelique's heart started to beat crazily. It was the first time she had tried *Semag*. She stood up, walked to the middle, and raised her right palm to the sky as if to demand everything from God. She lowered her left palm to the ground as if to share every benefaction received from the Lord with the others.

She started to whirl and lost all connections with her surroundings. She perceived Mevlana's shadow nearby. There were stars around her. She turned like the stars did and moved into a gleaming spot ahead of them. Some were disappearing in the bright cloud, but new ones were emerging.

Angelique went into the density of brightness. She witnessed shiny colors and whistles. Her soul felt ultimate peace and happiness. She saw flowers radiating the warmth of eternal love. She saw her mother and father. When their loving souls came together, they became brighter. Simon and Vahram joined them. They united as part of the densest light, and distinction was completely lost.

When things went dark, everything was lost. The tambourines stopped, and the *Semag* come to the end. Mevlana briefly prayed. They took their seats. Angelique was enchanted and could not speak for a while. There was a new horizon before her. She could now accept Suleiman Çelebi. The marriage would not be a betrayal of Simon. She realized that both souls were drops in the ocean of divine light. There was only one thing she still could not understand.

"Mevlana, my esteemed father, I realized a lot of divine secrets with your guidance. I lived my past and future at the same time. I understood that marrying Suleiman Çelebi would not be a betrayal of Simon, but I still do not understand one thing. When Kerra Hatun beat the tambourine the first time, my whole body trembled. Why have I been so affected?"

"That beat represented the first bang in the creation of the universe. It was the Word of the Lord to bring universe into existence. That's why you have been affected so much."

17

Love and Sorrow

Suleiman Çelebi and Angelique were married the following week. Mevlana gave them a small annex in his garden. Nothing—except moving to the new house—changed in their lives. Angelique was still serving Kerra Hatun, and Suleiman was playing and teaching tar. Angelique was happy beyond any expectations. Suleiman Çelebi was an extremely kind and sentimental man. He was always gentle with Angelique and tried his best not to upset her.

Kerra Hatun said, "Angelique, it has been two months since your marriage with Suleiman, but your abdomen is more enlarged. If you give birth before nine months, you will be a laughingstock. Your peaceful life will be distorted. I want you to leave Konya until you give birth and come back after a reasonable time."

"But where can we go, Kerra Ana?"

"Don't worry, Angelique. I shall send you to the house of ex-father-in-law in Larende. His nephews live there. Since they do not know when you married, they cannot gossip. We have also organized tar lessons for Suleiman at the Medrese. Help with the household when he is away. If you come back after nine or twelve months, all these problems will be solved."

Leaving Konya was difficult for Angelique at the beginning. Once more, she was leaving her loved ones. Although they would be back soon, she would still being deprived of Mevlana and Kerre Hatun's advice.

When they arrived in Larende, they were welcomed by Mevlana's nephews, Mehmet and Shemseddin, Çelebi, their wives, children, and servants. They were so friendly, that Angelique soon forgot the ones she had left in Konya. The men took Suleiman Çelebi, and the women took Angelique to show them round. Their room was much larger than the one in Konya. It had a fountain with running drinking water. The garden was full of fruit trees and beautiful flowers. Angelique could have spent her whole life here.

They had lunch by the garden pool. They felt like longtime family members. Some men took Suleiman to the Medrese to lecture about the tar. Soon, getting tar lessons from Suleiman was the fashion in Larende. The women loved Angelique's stories about Antioch.

Angelique's labor pains started on December 17, 1268. The most experienced doctor in the village was called. She gave birth to a healthy boy. After Suleiman Çelebi recited the name of God to Arif, it was Angelique's turn to take care of her baby.

The woman opened her breast close to the mouth, soft like silk.
A small and wet tongue touched her breast, full of milk.
Her baby knew his mother with the divine instinct of the Lord.
While his hands were grabbing mother's belly in accord,
Her motherly soul shivered with the touch of the baby.
A divine vibration had captured her completely.
It was not milk anymore flowing from her breast.
She transmitted the love she could give from her best.
She embraced her baby as if they were one being.
When she had been in love, she had not experienced this feeling.
In the wealthiest and the happiest times of her life,
She had not felt anything like the motherly strife.
In representing the God, a man she created.
This sacred job was to the women granted
And would never be known by males who are deprived of this feeling,

Intensified in the women, forced them to utmost caring.
Suddenly came to her mind the cost of divine bondage.
Her mother was victimized by her untimely courage.
Simon sacrificed himself for the sake of an unborn.
To a cruel Mongolian sword, Vahram stepped on.
Oh my God, how expensive the price of a child!
Why should the mothers suffer with the birth so very wild?
Is it not your order, Lord, in the world to give offspring?
Why should not men have the pain instead of with us sharing?

By the time Arif was turning one, he was crawling and trying to walk. He had yellow hair and blue eyes like his mother. He was the favorite of the Larende family. They celebrated his birthday as a big family.

Suleiman said, "Angelique, you do not look as happy as I expect to see you on our son's birthday. Is there something bothering you? Would you like to tell me something?"

"Suleiman Çelebi, I am sorry for our forgetfulness, for our ungratefulness. When Kerra Ana sent us here, she told us to return in five or six months after the birth, but what did we do? We forgot them all when we found comfort. If I had not met them, I would have died. Was my obligation to them so short?"

"Angelique, what a graceful heart you have. How lucky I am that God destined you to me. You are right. We should go back to Konya soon, but winter is not the proper time. The roads may be frozen. Arif may catch cold. I promise we will go in the spring."

"Thank you, Suleiman Çelebi. How lucky I am that I met such an understanding man. You have not broken my heart even once. You have treated Arif as your own child. If you want another one of your own, I am ready for that."

"No, Angelique. I won't. I do not trust myself. I am human. If I love a new baby more than Arif, I will not forgive myself of not keeping my word to Mevlana."

They stayed for three and a half more years. In the summer of 1273, bad news came from Konya. Mevlana was sick. They arrived in Konya the following week. Their annex had not been touched.

Kerra Hatun said, "Angelique I am pleased to see you. Your father missed you so much."

"Can we visit him right away? How is his health?"

"He is all right now. He will be pleased to see you."

Kerra Ana, Angelique, and Arif entered Mevlana's room. Angelique was pleased to see him on the couch instead of the bed. She ran to him, kissed him, and embraced him through her tears. She told Arif to kiss Mevlana's hands.

The old man took Arif on his lap. He looked at Angelique. "Where have you been, Angelique? I missed you so much. There are not many people around who kiss me and burst into tears."

"I am guilty, Father. We could not leave Larende."

"I know, Angelique. We went there with my father for seven months and stayed seven years. I found Gevher there—and you had Arif."

Suleiman entered and kissed his hands.

"Welcome, my son. After you left Konya, the *Semag* did not have the same spirituality. Nobody could play tar as well as you."

Angelique served Mevlana and Kerra Hatun all day long, carrying her son everywhere. Her arrival had a positive impact on Mevlana. He watched the flowers in the garden and listened to Arif.

"You know, Angelique, it's good you came. Our fading flowers have been revived. Our quiet garden has been cheered up by birds and a child's voice."

What a pity for those who look for God in seclusion.
Observing Mother Nature should be the real devotion.
Get in earthly beauties; colors and sounds are bound.
You cannot ascend to the sky without leaving the ground.

This seasonal happiness was as short as the summer rains. Mevlana's health worsened during the cold weather. He was unable to go out to the garden and spent most of his time in bed.

In the meantime, the citizens of Konya were in a panic from frequent earthquakes. "Oh great Mevlana, please pray that God will end these earthquakes."

"Don't be afraid, my boys. Soil wants a greasy body. When it gets this, everything will be calm."

The people left with new hope, but Angelique was sad because she had to leave her father.

Mevlana said, "Angelique, my girl, if I die, don't grieve for me. The day I die will be my wedding day to meet the eternal lover. If you have to leave Konya one day, don't give up because my grave was here. I will be buried in the hearts of lovers."

At last, the wedding day arrived. On December 17, 1273, Konya was crying. Carrying the coffin from the mosque to the cemetery took hours. People were reciting the Koran and the Bible at the same time.

Angelique saw a priest and said, "You are a Christian. Why do you cry?"

"Yes, I am, but Mevlana was closer to me than the patriarch or the pope. Who could explain the teachings of Christ better than Mevlana?"

Angelique stopped crying. Her father had died on the birthday of her son. His teaching proved that each death is a new birth.

18

Love and Sacrifice

T hree days after Mevlana's death, people returned to their normal lives. Angelique was busy preparing breakfast when three guards from the palace knocked on the door. They told Suleiman Çelebi about a call from Sahip Ata. He dressed and left home. In the palace, they took him directly to the regent.

"Welcome, Çelebi. We were all been shocked by the death of Mevlana. He was virtually my father as well. Now it is our duty to do a favor for him. You used to live in his house with your family. You may not stay there now. Just one day before Mevlana died, the head of the military band passed away. I recommended you to the sultan, and he accepted. Your duty will be to select and train the musicians, rehearse the pieces, and take care of administrative matters. You will be given an annex in the palace. Your son will be educated in the court school. What do you say?"

"His regency, it is an honor to be at the sultan's service. May I consult with my wife?"

"You are right. Talk to your wife and Kerra Hatun. Tell me your decision tomorrow."

At the turn of 1274, Angelique started in the court. She adapted to her new life quickly.

Arif had been accepted to the court school. His hard work made him a favorite among the teachers and his friends. At night, Suleiman Çelebi taught him to play the tar. In a short time, he showed much progress in music.

Angelique did not need to work. The palace women had loved her and accepted her as a friend. She did not gossip as most of the others did.

Hafize Hatun, the wife of Sahip Ata, learned how merciful she was against those who slandered her. The women knew all the details of her escape from Baybars.

In 1277, Mehmet Bey from Karamans cooperated with Baybars and attacked the Seljuks. They defeated the joint Karaman-Mongol armies in Elbistan and occupied Caesarion. The sultan and his viziers had to run away. There was only Sahip Ata in Konya.

Angelique thought about her strange destiny. Baybars was following her everywhere, but her worries did not last long. Baybars went to Egypt. He left part of his army in Karamanoglou. Mehmet Bey did not waste time and attacked and occupied Konya. He overthrew Sultan Gıyaseddin Keyhusrev and declared his nephew İzzeddin Keykavus as sultan and himself as the head of the viziers. Suleiman Çelebi conducted the military band for a new ruler. The changes affected Angelique and Suleiman Çelebi. They were not happy with their positions in the palace and the education of Arif.

One day Suleiman returned home early. Angelique had just prepared the dinner table. Çelebi attempted to sit, but he staggered with a pain in his leg and fell down. After some time, the stroke was over, but he could not move his leg. He wanted to hold his leg, but he could hardly even move his hand.

Arif rushed in and said, "What's wrong with you, Dad?"

They called the doctor. After a good examination, he said, "I am sorry, but Suleiman Çelebi is paralyzed on his right side. Thank God his left side is healthy. He can talk, breathe, and digest, but he cannot walk. He should be hospitalized."

Angelique said, "No! He will not go to the hospital. He cannot be away from his son and me. I shall take care of him at home."

The doctor said, "Then we should order a wheelchair for him."

"Please help us—and send it as quickly as possible."

The doctor prescribed some medicines, recommended some exercises, and left.

Suleiman Çelebi asked, "Angelique, darling, how are you going to take care of me?"

"My mother will not be alone. I shall stay and help her."

"You must attend your school, my son."

Arif put his arms around his neck. "I do not want to attend school, Dad. I want to stay by you."

"Okay. We will talk about it later. Eat and go to bed now."

Angelique helped Suleiman Çelebi get into bed. "Angelique, why are you so kind? You always take the difficult parts of life."

"I have learned that loving means sacrificing. My first husband, friends, and parents all sacrificed their lives for me. What I do for you is nothing compared to what they did for me."

Hard times started for Angelique. Suleiman needed continuous care. In order to afford a servant, buy food, and continue Arif's school, they needed money. Their savings were about to run out. The doctor had recommended hospitalizing him; all expenses would be covered by the state, but the treatment was very poor. Patients were left literally to die. Would Arif be permitted to continue his school with the new administration in Konya if Suleiman was no longer employed? How long could they keep their annex in the palace? The viziers, whose wives were the friends of Angelique, had stepped down. Who could help Angelique through this tough situation? Who could continue the same standards and not be affected by the changes?

She called Arif and said, "I have to be away for two hours. Please take care of your father."

––––––––––––––

When Tavus saw Angelique in her room at the Han, she embraced her. "Angelique, my sister, where have you been for so long?"

"I was afraid of not being recognized by you. Can you forgive me?"

"Forgive you? Crazy girl. I missed you so much that I was watching your way during the years. Tell me how you are. Does everything go well?"

Angelique said, "Till last week, things were all right. After Mevlana saved me from accusations, I married Suleiman Çelebi. We stayed in Larende for years. We had a son. My husband has been assigned as the bandmaster. We had a happy life. Unfortunately, my husband was paralyzed and lost his job. I could not send him to the hospital. I cannot afford to take care of his expenses with my savings. My son was a good student at the palace school, but his future at the school is unknown."

Tavus burst into tears.

Don't be misled, my sister, looking at me with tears.
They are, because I found you, reflections of my big cheers.
Don't ever think I am sorry for your miseries.
I will easily solve your troubles and queries.
Though you had forgotten me, I waited every day.
You were always in my heart, watching hopefully your way.
I was the first you recalled—what a pride it is for me.
I would give all my fortune that such a chance happened to be.

"Your old job is ready for you, Angelique. I shall give you a larger room to stay with your husband. Your son will have a separate one. Regarding his school, don't worry. He will continue. If you wonder about taking care of Suleiman, all my servants will be at his disposal."

Angelique looked at Tavus, pressed her head to her shoulder, and cried.

Don't be misled, my sister, looking at me with tears.
They are, because I found you, reflections of my big cheers.
I thought I lost Mevlana when he left the finite frame.
I see his eternal fire is always in the flame.
I was hopeless in the world with my husband and son.
I know now the Almighty would never leave me alone.

19

Hope of Happiness

Suleiman lost his health and job, but he was happier than ever. When he was head of the band, he had no time to spare for his family. Now his beloved wife was always by him. He was devoting more time to his son in tar and other lessons. He was eating and sleeping regularly. This regularity helped his recovery. He was forcing himself to move his right hand. He took a string in his right hand and practiced for hours. There was a visible progress in his health.

In September, Angelique and Suleiman were in their room.

Arif entered and said, "Mom, Dad, we took a test in Arabic. I got a certificate of achievement."

"Good, my boy. Let me see it." He looked at the paper and turned to his wife. "Angelique, what I got in four years, he achieved in three."

Suleiman, Çelebi, and Angelique were proud of Arif. Tavus was also happy.

Suleiman said "Son, bring my tar. I shall play a piece I composed for today."

Arif brought the tar and attached the string to his hand. Çelebi played with some difficulty. "Look—I can move my hand."

"Dad, your hand has recovered. I know your leg will also be all right."

"I believe that too. Miracles happen because of you and your mother's love."

Everybody was happy. Angelique said, "We shall always love you, Suleiman. We care so much about you."

Çelebi stopped using the wheelchair and started to walk with a crutch. He was quite encouraged. He believed in overcoming all difficulties with the help of his family.

20

Farewell to Earthly Life

The head of the palace guards, Emir-i Candar, came to the Han with two other soldiers.

Tavus was close to the gate and took them inside.

Emir-i Candar said, "Sahip Ata will be waiting for Suleiman Çelebi and his wife in the palace tomorrow."

Angelique said, "Tell the regent I shall be there with my husband."

In the morning, they went to the palace. They were taken to a private room instead of the reception hall.

Sahip Ata came in with his wife Hafize Hatun behind him. He said, "Suleiman, my son. Angelique, my daughter. I have been serving the Seljuk state and dynasties of sultans for forty years. I feel we have come to the end. I knew the sultanate would end when we lost Mevlana. After his death, nothing excites me. You are his heritage to me. I heard that your son finished court school. I do not want you to stay here anymore. I see the future of Anatolia is in the west. The unity and stability the Seljuks sought will be achieved by Ottoman Bey from the Kayi tribe. In order to encourage Ottoman Bey, our sultan decided to send him a military band. I assigned Arif to be the bandmaster. Tell him to come see me next week to get ready for the journey."

Suleiman Çelebi and Angelique thanked him. Sahip Ata left the room, but Hafize Hatun stayed.

There was a strange sadness at Ziyaeddin Han. Everybody had loved Suleiman Çelebi and his family. Nobody wanted them to leave, but everybody was unsure about the future.

Tavus ordered supper for the family. Suleiman Çelebi was on his way to the table with his crutches. He was very close to the table when a heavy stroke hit him. His crutches fell apart when he fell. They called a doctor immediately. His diagnosis was bad; the paralysis on his right side had worsened.

"I am sorry, Arif. I will not be able to go with you. Take your mother and go to Ottoman Bey."

"I will stay by you, Suleiman. Let Arif go alone."

"I will not go anywhere without my mother and father."

Once more, family ties forced them to sacrifice the future.

When Angelique went back to pick up the breakfast tray in the morning, she was terrified.

Suleiman Çelebi had sliced open his abdomen with a knife. There was a letter on the pillow.

A man with no child I was.
I knew Arif as my son.
No blood tie between us,
But I loved him like my own.
  He was born in winter cold.
  I cut his umbilical cord.
  I looked at him and adored.
  I said Arif he'll be named.
    He cried at certain times.
    I gave his milk in my arms.
    When he was sick or feeling bad,
    I waited near his bed.
      He cried when he fell in play.
      I felt his pain the same way.
      If he had an ache, I suffered.
      When I kissed him, his pain was over.

Fond of tar when he grew up,
In three years he learned Arab
And played tar as good as me.
I was paralyzed, but he stayed by me.
  Loving is more than other.
  Fathership is to labor.
  What stands as a hindrance?
  Sacrifice for son's favor.

A military band entered Ottoman Bey's territory. The women and children were in coaches and the men were on horses. When they passed a hill, they saw Sogut, the center of Ottoman Bey's reign. There were many tents on the green plain. This place was not alike Konya. There were no palaces or mansions close to Medrese. *Where were the children being educated? Would Arif's education be wasted?*

When they were close to the camp, the band members put on their official dresses. They took their instruments and marched toward a big tent. People woke up at once, got out of their tents, and watched the band curiously.

Arif stopped just before Ottoman Bey and signaled the band to stop the music. He gave a scroll to Ottoman Bey and said, "I am honored to bring you the firman of Seljuk sultan Giyaseddin Mesud."

Ottoman Bey took the scroll and looked at Arif. He liked this tall blond man. He opened the scroll and read the paper. He turned to his friends and said, "My veterans, courageous men, thank God we witnessed these days. The sultan recognized our ruling and sent us a military band to confirm it. Bandmaster, you took a long time. Introduce yourself."

"I am Arif, son of ex-bandmaster Suleiman. He died last week. I came with my mother."

Angelique stepped out of her coach and bowed. Ottoman Bey looked at her unmatched beauty.

"What is your name, *Hatun?*"

Without lifting up her head, Angelique said, "I am Angelique from

Antioch, Ottoman Bey. I ran away from the cruelty of Baybars and found refuge in Konya. Mevlana was my virtual father and made me marry Suleiman Çelebi. I had a happy life before Mevlana and my husband passed away. After my son graduated from Medrese, the sultan ordered us to join the band."

"You mean that Arif Çelebi is a Medrese graduate?"

"Yes, Ottoman Bey. He had his certificate in the best grade."

"Come to my tent with your son. I will introduce you to my children." He ordered his men. "The military band took a long way to come here. Take them to their tents. Arif Çelebi and his mother are my private guests. Prepare the big tent for them."

Arif and Angelique followed Ottoman Bey into his tent. Ottoman Bey showed them the seats on the couch near him. When everyone settled, he said, "Alaeddin and Orhan are my sons. My daughter Fatma is the eldest among my children. Arif Çelebi provides a great opportunity for us. I want him to take care of the education of my sons."

Arif stood and said, "Ottoman Bey, with your permission, I can prepare a program to start at once."

A month after their arrival, Angelique was familiar with the nomadic life. They were like a big family. People addressed each other with their own names. The horses in the folds and the cattle on the meadows were joint property. Angelique was called sister by everybody. Life was simple and far from gossip, lies, and intrigue.

Ottoman Bey's sons were respectful and loving toward Arif.

Angelique and Arif were usually the guests at Ottoman Bey's table at meals. At breakfast one morning, Ottoman Bey said, "Do you know how to ride, Angelique?"

"Yes, Ottoman Bey. I had a horse in Antioch."

"The weather is nice today. You have been here more than a month. Do you want to see the vicinage?"

Alaeddin and Orhan jumped up and said, "Can we come with you?"

"You can—if it does not coincide with your program. Arif, is there anything this morning?"

"Yes, Ottoman Bey. We will repeat Arabic letters."

"You can only ride in the afternoon. Tell Samsa to take you when you finish." Ottoman Bey turned to two of his men. "Aykut Alp, Turgut Alp, we shall show Angelique Hatun the places in close vicinity. Prepare the horses. Don't forget to take food and drinks."

After passing through the plain, they climbed to a hill that was covered by pine trees. From the plateau, they could see down to Sogut. There was a fountain with running spring water. It was a proper place to rest for lunch. The men prepared everything on the rug. All were hungry and ate with great appetites.

Turgut Alp and Aykut Alp approached Ottoman Bey and said, "It is hunting season here. Will you permit us to exercise our weapons?"

"I will—on the condition that you must be back before sunset."

Ottoman Bey and Angelique were alone. It was the first time she had seen him so closely. They must have been the same age. For a contemporary ruler, he could be considered young. In spite of that, he required respect from his people. He preferred listening; when he talked, his words they were so appropriate that everybody obeyed.

"Angelique, when you first came to Sogut, you said that you ran away from Baybars. What did you mean by his cruelty?"

"They sold young men and women in slave markets and killed the rest."

"They are wrong. We don't act like this."

"Then what do you do, Ottoman Bey? Is fighting not killing?"

"No, Angelique. Soldiers in battle kill or die. It's a matter of survival, but battles should not have any impact on civilians. When Seljuk Sultan Alpaslan came to Anatolia the first time, the number of Turks was not more than two hundred thousand. The Turkish identity in this land is stronger now. Most of them have converted to Islam. We didn't kill or sell the people on the lands we occupied because we wanted to stay permanently in Anatolia. We put the young men in the army as paid soldiers. We made the young girls marry our sons. The rest were free to select their religions. That is how we grew and became stronger."

Angelique was impressed by Ottoman Bey's words. Unlike Simon, he was aware of what he did and mobilized others.

Ottoman Bey said, "Don't be afraid—and do not move, Angelique."

Ottoman Bey's sword passed over her head and hit the ground. She turned in that direction. A poisonous snake had been split by the strike. Ottoman Bey almost fell on Angelique. He held Angelique's hand and sat near her. He put his hand around her neck and supported her head with his shoulder. "Don't worry, Angelique. When I am by you, I will protect you from all danger."

She trembled while Ottoman Bey was petting her hair. He looked at her beautiful blue eyes and soft hair. Angelique was strangely excited. She tried to resist, but her instincts had been pressed down for so long that she couldn't. She tried to stand; when she felt Ottoman Bey's lips on her neck, she reciprocated eagerly.

Ottoman Bey's passion for Angelique was so great that they began meeting almost every day. They would leave the embankment separately and meet at a designated place.

After a year of these meetings, Ottoman Bey said, "Angelique, we may not see each other for a week. We go fighting tomorrow."

"You mean you go to destroy, kill, loot, and confiscate."

"We confiscate—but not destroy or kill. If we destroyed or killed, we would not find anything next time. This is a two-sided deal. The Byzantine Empire and its magistrates attack our villages too, but they do not harm the people. Like us, they just loot."

"Is this not banditry, Ottoman Bey?"

"If I do it, it is called banditry. If the Romans and Persians do, it's heroism."

"Okay, Ottoman Bey, but Antioch never did such things. We were still the wealthiest country for 170 years. We encouraged trade and put levies on merchants."

"Angelique, if my grandchildren succeed in uniting the Anatolian people someday, there will be three reasons: Arif's lectures to my sons, your suggestions to me, and our proximity to the Byzantine Empire.

I will do once more what you have inspired me to do. I will set up marketplaces in Sogut and put levies on the vendors."

"I understand the first two but cannot grasp the third. Why do you find it useful to be the neighbor of a strong empire?"

"Having a strong neighbor is a risk for you—and for your enemies. It serves as a shield for you. Byzantium is strong, but they are not cruel people like the Mongols or Mamluks. Moreover they are not as strong anymore."

Ottoman Bey and his soldiers came back after a week. They had beaten the Inegol and Karacahisar magistrates near Domanic. Everyone welcomed them cheerfully. There was a lot of loot to be distributed. They helped carry the injured soldiers to the doctor and embraced their men.

Ottoman Bey's nephews encircled him and said, "Uncle, where is our father? We do not see him."

"My Sarubati brother fought valiantly and was a martyr. God bless him." He embraced them and tried to console them. He then took the floor, told the fight to the public, and mentioned the names of the fallen. He separated 20 percent of the loot for the sultan. That left his share, 20 percent for his nephews, and the rest to his people. Angelique and Arif also got a share since they were considered citizens.

———————

There was excitement in Sogut in the spring of 1291. Arif and Alaeddin had learned reading and writing in Arabic and would get certificates from their teacher. Everybody gathered in the square.

Ottoman Bey said, "Alaeddin, come here. Take the Koran and read the page I open."

He did the same with Orhan and his other son completed the same achievement.

"My dear citizens, I do not know if there is a bigger source of pride for a father. I cannot pay my debt to Arif. I will ask him to accept a purse full of Byzantine gold coins. What I am going to tell my sons—except that I will never forget. You will always respect Arif and consult him when there is something you cannot solve. You should always support each other and never act against. If one day you are the head of our state, don't forget to establish the following institutions: courts to make justice, guards to provide security, schools for enlightenment, and a military for endurance."

The people understood that they would need more than victories on battlefields to be a state. There were many years ahead before independence. When Karacahisar attacked the Turkish villages, Ottoman Bey and his soldiers had to go fighting. They band went with them. The remaining had to wait anxiously for their return. It did not take long for the anxiety to be replaced by celebrations. Karacahisar had been conquered.

A messenger told them of the victory and Ottoman Bey's plan to stay in Karacahisar for administrative organizations. He requested the presence of Orhan, Arif, and Angelique. When they arrived, Ottoman Bey said, "My son, veterans, thank God we have come to these days. The death of Yavsak Aslan, the ruler of our Turkish neighbor, and the conquest of Karacahisar forced us to make plans to strengthen and reorganize our justice, security, and education establishments. I give Orhan this fortress to put our plans into implementation with his master, Arif Çelebi."

Angelique, Arif, and Orhan settled in Karacahisar permanently. Ottoman Bey wanted to visit the churches to see if his soldiers had harmed them. He asked Angelique to accompany him. They rode horses to the greatest church in the fortress.

The priest welcomed them at the gate. Angelique walked to the Virgin Mary statue and prayed. When she turned her head, Ottoman Bey was kneeled and praying too. The priest was watching in amazement.

Ottoman Bey said, "Don't get confused. If this place is the temple of God—and if we all are his supplicants—everybody should be able to pray to the same God at the same place in different languages. Could I be the founder of an empire if I had not shown this tolerance? Besides, my father and ancestors were Shamanist when they first came here."

Angelique said, "No, Ottoman Bey. I am not confused. Mevlana once said: *In the fetish of shaman in statues of Mary. What you pray in the church and the mosque is from God.*"

Ottoman Bey and the priest were not expecting such words from Angelique.

In the priest's room, Ottoman Bey said, "Do you have any complaints about my soldiers or any other problems?"

"Not at all. None of your soldiers disturbed us. My sole problem is the oldness of the church, which had not been repaired for a long time. We have no funds to fix it."

"Don't worry. This church will be repaired soon. Your worship will continue with no hindrance, but can you help me solve a problem?"

"Oh my God. It will be the greatest honor if a poor man like me can help you."

"You can—but can you keep my secret as well?"

"I will take your secret to the grave with me."

"Listen. I love this lady, but she is a Christian. I am Muslim. We cannot get married officially. I do not want us to feel any guilt because of our relationship. Will you marry us before God?"

Angelique was surprised, happy, and excited. They returned to the magistrate's palace in the evening. Nobody noticed anything, but they had completely new personalities.

In the spring of 1298, Angelique was waiting for Ottoman Bey in the palace. They had been together for more than ten years. After she moved to Karacahisar, their meetings were much easier. Ottoman Bey was coming to the palace to see his son, and they were getting together secretly at the night.

Ottoman Bey said, "Angelique, my love, the most exciting moment of my life was when I first met you. I lived my happiest times with you. I always loved you—and I will forever—but I am afraid the time has come for sacrifice. Do you remember how I declared our independence after the conquest of Karacahisar? We are on the verge of an important announcement. The chance to proclaim an Ottoman state is before us."

"I am very pleased with that, but what's that got to do with our relationship?"

"In order to establish a state and keep it going, I need strong supporters. The most influential person in this area—the one all Turkomans obey—is Sheikh Edebali. If I can get him on my side, my plan will work easily. The one way to achieve this is by marrying his daughter, Bala Hatun. Unfortunately, if it happens, we cannot meet again. I will have to bury my eternal love in my heart."

Angelique wanted to cry—but could not do it. "Don't be sorry, Ottoman Bey. If humans can live peacefully in your state, it's worth our separation. If men and women from different races and religions can approach each other in limitless tolerance, I am ready to sacrifice my happiness. Anyway, what does it mean to be a woman other than lifelong sacrifices? Each time she gives birth, there is a risk of death, but women dive into danger gladly. The greatest burden—to raise a baby—falls on woman. She accepts it with no complaints. In some marriages, men torture women. She bears it patiently, but if her man gets sick, she waits by his bed. In battles, men die easily. The women are tortured, raped, and humiliated in the slave markets, but if her man returns as victor, she accepts her husband's marriage to others to crown his victory. How lucky I was that I met two of the most influential men of the thirteenth century. I saw the fall and rise of the states, but I confess that the longest happiness I found was in you, Ottoman Bey."

There were tears in Ottoman Bey's eyes. Would a love at this magnitude be sacrificed for anything else? History had given him a responsibility. "Angelique, I wish I had no responsibility for others and could live happily with you for the rest of my life. How can I disregard those who are murdered, raped, looted, or starved on this land with no hope for the future for themselves or their children? Our children will live together on this land. I don't want them to suffer from separation as we did. I still consider myself the happiest man of my time. I have loved you for so many years."

The lovers embraced a final time.

In the spring of 1299, the Bilecik magistrate who was to marry the daughter of Yarhisar invited Ottoman Bey and his men to his wedding festivity. In the spring the Sogut people migrated to Domanic plateau until autumn. Ottoman Bey asked to leave all his belongings at the Bilecik castle before coming to the wedding.

It was the usual practice in those years to entrust the heavy goods of encampment to neighboring castles. The magistrate accepted gladly. The wedding would be in Chakirpinar, two hours away from Bilecik.

On the way to the wedding, the magistrate of Yarhisar was encircled by Ottoman Bey's soldiers. They turned back toward Yarhisar. When the people saw their magistrate, they opened the gates—and Ottoman Bey's soldiers got in. The conquest of the castle did not take long.

At the Bilecik castle, one of the bales left by Ottoman Bey was opened. A soldier got out of it and informed others. Armed soldiers stepping out of the bales captured everyone in the castle. Bilecik had fallen to the Ottomans. While the guests were waiting for the bride, the horsemen of the Ottomans appeared.

"Good news, Ottoman Bey. Both Bilecik and Yarhisar castles were conquered."

There was a big ceremony in Karacahisar. Orhan Bey would marry Holofira, the daughter of the Yarhisar magistrate. The young bride converted to Islam and became Nilufer Hatun.

After the ceremony was over, Ottoman Bey said, "Citizens, veterans, sisters, warriors, and Turkomans, we are gathered here to celebrate two important events. The first one is the wedding of Orhan and Nilufer. The second will make all of us happier than the first one. I proclaim the foundation of the Ottoman state. That is my wedding present to Orhan and all of you. Ottomans will survive for centuries and give happiness to all humankind without any discrimination of race, religion, or color. Under the Ottoman reign, citizens will always be safe. As long as we follow the path of wisdom and science, no one can stop us. If we deviate from the truth and cannot adapt ourselves to the changes, we may fall.

I want to lay down the fundamentals of Ottomans with the advice of my father-in-law, the wisest man of our time."

Sheikh Edebali stood up walked toward Ottoman Bey. He said, "Son, you are the ruler now and have taken command. From now on, anger is for us—and calmness is for you. If we are crossed, you will be the reconciler. If we become arrogant, you will be humble. If we fail, accuse, or make mistakes, you will correct. Disputes, bad temperaments, and disagreements are for us, mediation, understanding, and kindness are for you. You will forgive even the most malicious ones. We shall be dividing—and you will be completing. We shall be lazy, and you will be industrious. If we are discouraged somewhere, you will encourage us. Stay alive so the people of your state can survive. Your task is difficult. God help you."

Angelique watched Arif lead the military band as it played for the cheering crowd. Suddenly, she felt a pain in her leg. The snake had followed her for years, saved her from slavery and got Ottoman bey for her had finally accomplished the divine task. She tried to scream, but nobody heard her. She had difficulty breathing. She knew she was dying, but there was a smile on her face.

When Angelique woke up in the realm of divine light as the Great Angel, she remembered both lives. How clever was it to experience human life. Humans had been destined to join divine spirituality at the end.

Oh my God, I thank you for your benevolence to me.
You destined me in life—both artist and mother to be.
Your creation power in myself manifested .
All my earthly works your inspiration reflected.
Then I was born as woman sacrifices I tended.
To absolute sea of love with Semag I ascended.
With colors and voices, my soul enchanted at the end.
To the great Mevlana, you made me a loyal friend.
Grateful to you, I think finished my evolution.
Reaching your divine heaven is my only petition.

The Great Angel perceived the divine appeal of Lord:
Oh my angel, you have wished to be a human in the world
And experience human evolution of the Lord.
Thus you have learned the secrets of divine creation.
Your evil and good deeds won your examination.
The position you earned is omnipotence.
You create your heaven with your mind and with your sense.
Whatever you dream of in your heaven, you will find.
Whoever you want to see will be there as humankind.
You will get all your power here direct from me.
With your loved ones near, you will exist eternally.

The Great Angel was not satisfied with this. He felt something was missing. He wanted to see the Lord in a personalized form. He reflected his wish in his thoughts.

Oh my God, if you won't be, what should I do with heaven?
Can I be satisfied with what I have already seen?
I knew all my beloved ones when I everywhere lived on earth.
Why should I need your power if we won't meet somewhere?

The Great Angel was scared of these thoughts. Was it disrespectful to the Lord? But all worries were invalidated.

You used to see me on earth, but you never recognized.
You enjoyed all my potions, not knowing I realized
I was the source of your art and knowledge.
I inspired your merits and the sacrifices you made.
All substances in the universe are manifested by me.
All incidents on the earth are simply my destiny
I personalized in you and appeared in two persons:
First dressed up as an artist and then as motherly icons.
If you still do not get it, you must know better and more.
You are the human form of me in divine mirror.

At that moment, a blinding light covered everything. Never had the Great Angel perceived such brightness. In the middle of the light, some spots darkened. The spots formed a figure as they would on a mirror. When the figure became recognizable, the Great Angel knew it was a personification of God. It was nobody else but Angelique.